THE GHOST HUNTER

THE GHOST HUNTER

STEVE ALTIER

DCB

DARK CLOUD BOOKS

Imprint: Dark Cloud Books

ISBN: 978-1-0878-9600-7

Printed in the United States of America.

Books by Steve Altier

Young Adult Novels:

Lizardville, The Ghost Story

Lizardville Jimmy's Curse

The Ghost Hunter

Middle-Grade Stories:

We Can't Move at Christmas

Gabby and Maddox Adventures in Italy

Blast Off with Gabby and Maddox

Gabby and Maddox Activity Book

"Coming Soon"

Over The Falls with Gabby and Maddox

CHAPTER ONE

The battle raged on, the fight for life or death. One hung on, doing everything in his power to survive. Pulling and tugging, they continued to fight. Pieces of meat were ripped off with all the thrashing back and forth. One of the two combatants desperately tried to hide in the tall grass. The larger one grabbed and ripped the other's flesh, while the weaker one curled up, trying to defend himself. It was a losing battle.

I sat, shocked, amazed, and speechless, my mind racing as the events unfolded before my eyes. My heart was pounding like a big bass drum and for a moment, I thought it would bounce out of my chest. I had never witnessed anything like this before. Should I do something? What could I do? I was only a child.

I gazed to my right, watching the bees buzz in the nearby flowers. I caught a whiff of jasmine as the wind blew in my direction, and the soft flowery scent filled my nose. I took it all in. The flowers were my mother's favorite, and they were in full bloom. The bees went on about their business, oblivious to the battle taking place a few yards away. I glanced to the left—nothing but a row of trees lined the driveway. What should I do? Watch? Interfere? My mind raced, thoughts bouncing around my head like a ping pong ball in a closed box. I sat motionless, unsure of what course of action to take. This wasn't something I could solve by searching a textbook. No, this was something I would have to figure out on my own.

Time slowed down, every second lasting an eternity in this fight for survival. I watched as the worm hung on for its life and the other tried to fend off starvation. The worm clung onto whatever it could; the bird pulled and ripped, piece by piece, as it slowly devoured its prey. The battle finally ended, one happy with a full belly, and the other, gone, wiped off the face of the earth. My nerves rattled; my hands trembled. Nature was brutal but had taken its course. The battle was over, and the bird had won. I never doubted it would. How fast things can end. One moment the worm was waking up, minding his own business, crawling out of his hole to welcome the new day, and the next second, it was over. I wondered what went through your mind as you took your last breath. I just hope I'm old and gray before I die.

I didn't know how I felt, maybe perplexed? Part of me was thinking how cool it was that I had been able to witness nature at its finest. Was I wrong to think this way? The other side of my brain said it was disgusting. I guess that really depends on whether you're the bird or the worm. The scene challenged me, and I drifted off to another time when I had lost my puppy. I never knew what happened to him. Mommy said he ran away. I wondered if that was true or if she had decided to return him to the pet store. Or had she done something unthinkable? I loved that little runt, even though I only had him for a few weeks. Was he still alive? Was he living a good life? I wish I knew.

I often think about that day as I go through life. I was ten years old when I witnessed that murder. It's a day that will be etched into my mind forever. I often look back at my life the same way, yet I'm always the worm—the one who's being picked on by others. I dislike bullies. When you have a name like mine, of course, all the kids are going to make fun of you. I'm Gerald, but that's not the bad part since a lot of kids have that name. No, I'm Gerald, Gerald Dupickle. See the problem? Pickle head, pickle boy, green pickle, green machine . . . you name it, I've heard it.

Did I mention I was smarter than the other kids, too? I also took advanced classes in high school. I was the smallest kid in school, and I was a few years ahead of my age group. Then throw in the name, and that made me one easy target.

My mother, Lydia, did all she could to protect me when I was younger. She always called the other moms and complained about the boys who beat me up or tossed my backpack up into a tree. I begged her to stop calling, it only made matters worse, but she never listened to me. The older I became, the less I told her about my problems.

See? Even I can learn from my mistakes.

I guess if I had a father or even knew my dad, it might have made a difference. Maybe he would have taught me how to fight or defend myself, or at least block a punch. Ah, who am I kidding? I was clumsy with a capital C. The awkward kid in the class, it made me think life wasn't fair—I had plenty of book smarts yet no street smarts. Someone played a cruel joke on me. But that's life, and you can't change who you are—believe me, I've tried.

Over the years, I have learned to embrace who I am. I even like who I am, but I always wondered what it would be like to be part of the cool crowd—the person who everybody loved, the guy the other kids wanted to be and hang out with, the sports hero who won the game at the final buzzer. The girls would all want to flock to me. Maybe I would even have a girlfriend. But that wasn't going to happen. That's right, I was still the worm fighting for survival.

Then things changed, and my wish came true . . . well, sort of. The house next door sat empty for a long time. An investor purchased the home, fixed it up, and sold it for a profit. Smart move, if you ask me.

A new family moved in, and that's when I met Bates Bergen. Bates and I sort of became friends. Bates was older than me and twice my size, but not very smart. Bates offered me protection if I would help him with school. That worked for several years, and over time, we formed a pretty good friendship. But like many things in life, it expired. Things change, times change, and people go in different directions. Even though I promised to write, I hope he keeps in touch.

That pretty much sums up my childhood. Now I'm starting college. It's my first day, and I have to admit, I'm nervous. My stomach ached, felt twisted, like a dozen butterflies flying around. I only hoped I wouldn't retch in front of everyone. That would doom me before I even had a chance to be one of the cool kids.

That's right, I won't stop trying. That's what people say: 'Never give up.' I don't know or understand why I want to fit in so badly. Maybe it's because I never have. You see, we always want what wc can't have.

So, here I am, a freshman in college at the age of sixteen. Who wouldn't want to hang out with me? I've grown over the years, and now many kids have to look up when we talk, so I look older than I actually am. However, I could stand to gain some weight. I avoid sunlight as much as possible—it's not good for my skin. My blonde hair always looks messy because it's hard to do anything with all these curls. My best feature is my smile, or so my mother and aunt have always told me. So, what's not to love, right? Maybe it's my lack of people skills—or so I've been told.

I stared out the window as Mom rounded the bend, the college coming into view. The three to four-story buildings looked grand. The red bricks told a story in themselves—the dark-colored bricks looked aged. Instantly, I knew those buildings had been here for decades. Then there were buildings made with lighter-colored bricks, which had to be relatively new, maybe built in the last three to five years.

Wait. Do other students think like this?

Mom slowed down as we approached the black, wrought-iron gates. Lock Haven University was stenciled over the entrance. She chose this university for me. It would not have been my first choice, especially since there were others I had my eye on, but they were larger schools.

The campus was located in a small Pennsylvania town overlooking the Susquehanna River—that's an Indian name if I ever heard one. The school bore the same name as the town. I guess my mom felt I would be safer attending a small college, hidden and tucked away from the world.

She smiled through the rearview mirror. "We're almost there."

I half-smiled back; yes, she still made me ride in the back. Another embarrassing fact, she felt I was safer in the backseat. After all, it was the late 1960s and our car didn't have anything called seatbelts.

The registration paperwork stated fewer than four thousand students attended the school annually. I loved facts. I wondered how many parents and students have passed underneath this entryway. It wouldn't take long to figure it out if I did the math. Mom turned her blinker on before making a slow, left-hand turn onto Eagle Lane. Our school mascot was the flying eagle, so it only made sense to have the main road named after it.

We passed one of the older buildings on our right, Mason Hall—the science center. That's where I planned to spend most of my time. My excitement level rose a notch and my eyes grew wide. The building reminded me of an old turn of the century palace. It stretched for an eternity. I couldn't wait to step inside and breathe in the rich history.

I quickly noticed the large windows that spanned across the entire four stories of the Nelson Center. My mouth fell open. I gawked at the racks of books as we drove passed. Row after row of books appeared on every floor.

Oh my, I gushed, *I'm going to love this library.*

I flew forward, crashing into the seat in front of me.

"Are you okay, baby?" Mom bellowed.

"I'm fine, and stop calling me baby," I begged and searched for my glasses on the floor.

"But you are my baby, and you always will be." She smiled and turned her attention to the group of boys crossing the street in front of us. She cranked her window down slightly. "This isn't a crosswalk," she howled.

I took cover behind the seat, once again hiding from the world. That's the last thing I needed—a large target pasted on my back. *Oh look, here comes the kid whose mother yells at students walking in the streets.*

I heard one of them holler as we passed, and I caught a glimpse of his rude and all-too-common hand gesture.

"Your mother needs to teach you some manners," she threatened.

"Mom, will you please move on?" I whimpered from the floorboard.

"I don't need your snide remarks," she scolded me. The car lunged forward as we continued down Eagle Lane. I crouched low in the backseat. I couldn't wait to get out of the car and be free of her. It's times like these that I wish I had a father. I'm sure he would have been cool and told her to relax, then he would probably wave at the boys, who would have waved back. He would have been the kind of father everyone wanted . . .

He would have been my best friend.

Mom turned right down the lane toward the college dorms. They were nestled in the center of the campus, giving easy access to all of our classes, and everything was within walking distance. The newest building towered before us as the car slowly came to a stop. Decan Hall, the freshman dormitory building and the place I would call home for the next year. Each year I would have to move to a new building. I never understood that; *wouldn't it be easier to stay in the same location every year?* I'm sure there was a reason for it though, one I couldn't wrap my head around at the moment.

The door screeched open as Mom stepped out of the car. I rose and peered out the window. *Everything is going to be okay*. I pulled the handle and pushed open the door. A new world awaited. I placed a foot outside and stepped into the fresh, crisp mountain air. I looked around. The other students were doing the same—getting out of vehicles and looking around, many as lost as I was, and for the first time, I didn't feel alone. We were all lost.

Boys and girls bustled about carrying luggage and boxes into the building. The trunk sprang open, and Mom instructed me to grab my bags. I wrapped my hand around the handle and removed the bag from the trunk.

Snap.

Pop.

I watched the contents of my suitcase spill all over the ground. Others stopped, looked, laughed . . . it was high school all over again. Not the entrance I'd planned on making. T-shirts, underwear, and socks galore, I scurried to grab them as quickly as possible, trying not to make eye contact with anyone. Mom leaned forward to help.

"I got this," I snapped.

"Excuse me," she screamed. "How dare you bark at me?"

Things were going from bad to worse in seconds. "Mom, I'm sorry. Please, calm down. I don't need a scene, please!" I begged.

She softened and gave me one of her half-smiles. "Okay, I'll let you handle this."

I jammed the last piece of clothing into the bag and snapped the lid shut. I raised my head to notice if anyone seemed to care. Everyone kept walking.

Huh, maybe college was going to be different.

I stood and wrapped both arms around the bag and started toward the door with Mom on my heels. I then spotted a few older boys standing along the block wall next to the park wearing blue jeans and black T-shirts—a stark contrast to the plaid button-up shirt and brown corduroy pants I was wearing. They pointed and laughed, and I was sure they were calling me all sorts of things.

Ugh, maybe this was like high school all over again . . .

CHAPTER TWO

I lugged my broken suitcase up three flights of stairs. I was glad I didn't get the room on the fourth floor, even though I had fussed about not getting the place I wanted—which was typical of me to raise a stink about not getting my way. Winded, I pushed the door open and looked down the corridor. It was times like this that I longed to be more athletic, but most book nerds, like me, were not inclined to take up sports. I started down the hallway—303 the number pasted on the middle of the brown door. I glided a little farther to 305. I moved past lucky 307, and then stopped and stared at my door, number 309. Why couldn't I have lucky Room 307? But it was time to be a man and accept the room I was given, which was, sadly, 309.

"Why are you waiting? These boxes are heavy," Mother blurted out.

"Sorry." I set my bag down and pulled the metal key from my pocket, slid it into the slot, turned, and shoved the door open. Dorm sweet dorm, this was my new home. The room was larger than I had expected. The walls were bare, but the room contained all the proper furnishings—two beds, two small wooden desks with chairs, and a chest of drawers for each of us.

"Hello."

Startled, I blinked and gazed to the far side of the room. "Ah, hello," I said in a sheepish voice to the young man sitting on the bed near the window.

He pointed to his chest and smiled. "I'm Kim Lu, your roommate."

Kim was an Asian boy, shorter than me by a few inches, thin and bony like myself. He even wore glasses. Things were looking up. I'd never met any Asian kids. My mother sheltered me growing up. *This might work out well.* I heard or read somewhere that Asian children were brilliant; maybe we could study together. He may even challenge me on an intellectual level. "Hi, I'm Gerald Dupickle." I smiled.

"Are you going to introduce me?" Mother cut in.

"Sorry." I pointed to my mom. "This is Lydia."

"Lydia?" Her tone said it all. "I'm Gerald's *mother*. He's ashamed to call me mom." She glared at me with her look.

"Sorry, Mom." I bowed my head and noticed Kim had done the same. I had the feeling he knew what I was going through. I Wondered if maybe he'd grown up in a similar environment, one with strict rules and a lack of fun? Perhaps he even came from a broken home like mine? My mind wandered as I sat the suitcase on the bed closest to the door. I wanted the bed farthest from the door—I had always had this phobia about being closest person to the door—but didn't want to start off on the wrong foot with my new roomie, so I kept my mouth shut.

Kim and I didn't say much. He watched as I made several trips back and forth, bringing up a few boxes at a time. I wondered why he didn't offer to help. Maybe it was my mother, or the fact that I hadn't been here to help him bring his stuff in the room.

Finally, the last of my things were in place. Mother grabbed me and gave me a long hug. I wanted her to be gone and get on with this new chapter in my life. But she held me tight, and whispered things that my roommate could hear. "I love you bunches. You have fun and study hard. Don't forget to brush your teeth three times a day. Get a bath before you go to bed and make sure you get to sleep by nine-thirty every night, unless it's Saturday . . . then you can stay up until ten. You know how you get if you don't get enough sleep."

I half grinned, my face red with embarrassment. "I will Mom, I promise," I said with the hope that she would leave before she said anything else that would embarrass me. I felt fortunate that Kim kept his back to me. I think he understood how I felt.

"I love you too, Mom." Then she kissed me on the cheek. I watched as a tear traced down the side of her face. I smiled. There's no greater love than a mother's love.

She turned and never looked back as she walked out the door and softly closed it behind her.

Relief flooded me. I lowered myself and sat on the edge of my bed.

"What would you like to do?"

I hadn't noticed Kim staring at me. "What do you have in mind?" I asked.

"I thought we could go check out the campus."

What a great idea. I walked to the window and caught a glimpse of my mother getting into her car, then slowly driving away. "Sure, that sounds great." I figured I could unpack later.

I felt the metal key in my right front pocket and my wallet in the other. I was ready and started for the door. I didn't say much, and neither did Kim as we walked down the stairs and out the front door. We stopped, looked left and then right. Kim nodded to the right, so that's the direction we went.

"Ah look, it's suitcase boy and his tighty-whitie undies," some boys hollered and laughed. I'd forgotten all about them sitting on the wall. Kim scurried away, and I picked up my pace to match his. The group jumped off the wall and followed. I could hear them chuckle as we walked. Where's Bates when I needed him? But he wasn't here to protect me anymore. Kim walked faster and I tried to keep up, but it felt like we were sprinting. I could tell he had experience with running from trouble. It takes a nerd to know a nerd.

We rounded the corner and down the next street, the sound of their footsteps closing in on us. Nelson Center Library came into view. *We could duck in there*. Kim must have read my mind and started for the door. I stopped before going inside, turned, looked, and much to my surprise, no one was following us. The street was empty. It didn't make sense. No one followed us. Had I imagined that? Maybe college was going to be different. I smiled, turned, and gazed at all the books as I entered.

The librarian sat behind her desk and cracked a smile at us. I followed Kim down the central aisle, glancing at all the rows of books. Kim started up the stairs to the second floor, then stopped on the third. I guess he knew where he was going. I followed him to the back of the room, and as we rounded the final row of shelves, I noticed several empty tables. Kim grabbed a book and took a seat. I guess he already knew what he wanted to read.

This floor was empty, except for Kim and me. I got the feeling we were hiding from someone, but that didn't add up since the other boys didn't follow us. Less than an hour at college and I already felt like I was back in high school.

Might as well make the best of it. I walked to the closest aisle, wanting to touch and feel and yes, even smell every book. I noticed something move out of the corner of my eye. *That was strange* . . . One of the books inched forward. I knew I was alone. I looked left, then right. I stared at the book again, which had stopped moving. My mind must be playing tricks on me. I glanced at Kim sitting at the table, his head buried in a book. Startled, I jumped as the book slapped the tile floor. Eyes wide, I gazed at the book. "Shh," Kim whispered as he must have thought I dropped it.

I bent over and wrapped my long fingers around the book. "Do You Believe in Ghosts?" by Lance Edwards. *What?* I looked around without standing as I gawked at the cover. *Do I believe in ghosts?* I smiled. *Of course not.* Kim must have led me here to play a trick on me. Wow, maybe I have a fun roommate. My grin grew wide, I was on to his game. I straightened up and placed the book back on the shelf where it belonged.

Another thunderous crack echoed. A second book had dislodged itself from the shelf. "Shh!" Kim scolded.

Puzzled, I took a step in the direction of the fallen book. I froze; all I could do was look at the cover. "Proof that Ghosts Exist." I scuttled back, suppressing a shiver. What was going on? I looked at the sign at the end of the aisle. *Paranormal.*

Why had Kim brought me to the paranormal section of the library? Who else was here? No one from what I could see; it was only the two of us.

"This isn't funny," I whispered to Kim.

He shot me a puzzled look before he shushed me again.

Slowly another book began to inch its way forward. Paralyzed, I watched. This is impossible. Everyone knows ghosts are only stories passed down from generation to generation. They were far from real, yet the book continued to move. I lunged forward and extended my hand. My most significant moment in sports history would be catching this falling book. I watched as it skimmed my fingertips and crashed to the floor.

"Be quiet," Kim insisted.

Mortified, I glanced at the tiled floor where the cover lay face down. That wasn't good; now I would have to know what the cover read. Frozen in fear, I looked at the book for a few moments as I grappled with what to do. My body twisted and squirmed inside. I was feeling too much like the worm who was about to be devoured. *I couldn't just leave the book like this, could I?* I should walk away, go back to my dorm, and leave the book lying on the floor. Yes, that was an option, one I could not follow through with. I couldn't just leave it on the floor. It had to go back where it belonged, which meant I had to touch the book.

I heard a soft chuckle. What? I stilled myself as I heard another faint hint of laughter. It came from the next aisle over and sounded feminine. I wasn't alone. I cocked an eyebrow. My throat clicked when I swallowed as I moved to the end of the row. Stealth mode was never a strong suit of mine—I was clumsy and awkward in moments like this. I breathed in and placed a hand on the end of the bookshelf. Slowly, I forced myself to peek around the corner. I blinked, not once but several times. The aisle was empty. I was disappointed because logically, books could not move by themselves and I knew I heard giggles. I appraised the situation. Someone had to be behind this, yet the row was empty. Things weren't adding up, and anyone who knew me understood that numbers had to add up.

Frustrated, I sighed, inhaled, and tried to relax. Pivoting on my heels, I spun around and lunged backward. "Who are you and where did you come from?" I hollered.

"Shh," she whispered and raised a finger to her mouth to shush me. Kim gazed at us from the table with wide eyes; I'm not sure he could speak. He, like myself, didn't have a lot of experience talking to girls. She softly chuckled, holding the book in her hand. I noticed the cover, "How to Catch a Ghost."

"I didn't mean to scare you . . . I was only playing around." Her voice was soft and sweet to my ears. I'd never heard anything so kind.

"Ah, hi-ya."

She cocked her head to the side, confused. "Ah, hi-ya?"

My heart galloped, and I angled my head to the floor. She wore pink sneakers and nice blue jeans. Her legs were long, and she had a tight waistline. Sweat started to bead on my forehead. *Please don't let my glasses fog over*. Panic was about to set in when she spoke.

“Are you okay? I honestly didn’t mean to scare you. I feel bad. Do you want to sit?” She steered me to the nearest table and wrapped her hand around my arm to steady me.

I almost pulled away, but her hand was warm and soft against my skin, so I let her guide me. I pulled out a chair and lowered myself down. She grabbed a chair and slid it next to mine. *I’m such a dummy. I should have pulled the chair out for her.* I wanted to apologize for my actions, but my lips didn’t move.

Her hand moved up to my shoulder, and she pushed me back slightly. “Do you feel better?”

My eyes moved upward to where her long blonde hair cascaded like waves in an ocean. She could have been a model. I’d only seen girls this pretty in magazines. She had the prettiest blue eyes. I was hypnotized. I knew right away she was out of my league. My head bobbed up and down to let her know I was feeling better.

“So, you’re okay?”

I nodded again.

“I’m Angela, but my friends call me Angel,” she whispered. “This is Deidre,” she pointed to the gal standing behind her I hadn’t even noticed, “but we call her Dee for short.”

Dee issued a shy wave. I knew the minute I saw her; she was the gal for me. Her red high heels, tight blue jeans, brunette hair, olive-toned skin, and those spellbinding brown eyes hidden behind brown-framed glasses. She wore bright red lipstick, and her smile was contagious. I knew I was going to hyperventilate. Struggling to calm my breathing, I bent over and placed my hands on my knees.

"Wow, Dee," Angel giggled, "you took his breath away."

"Do you have a name?" Dee asked as she stepped forward.

"Gerald," I whimpered from between my knees. Angel laid her hand on my back and rubbed in a circular motion. It felt like something my mother would have done for me. Gradually, I raised my head to look at the two ladies before me. "I'm okay," I managed to say with my hands propped on my thighs.

Thrusting her shoulders back slightly, Dee raised a hand and gently pushed her hair back, tucking a long stand behind her ear. *Was she flirting with me?* My mouth agape, I gazed at Kim, who was sitting alone on the other side of the room. He scratched his chin and appeared as baffled as I was. He parted his lips, trying to mouth something to me, but I had no clue what he was trying to say.

"Are you a freshman, Gerald?" Angel asked.

"Yes," I pushed out. "I'm staying in the freshman dorm." The minute the words left my mouth, I knew they sounded idiotic. To my surprise, the girls didn't seem to care. I blushed and smiled.

"I'm a sophomore, and Dee's a junior."

Dee looked young, yet she was older. Twenty, if I had to guess. I felt she would freak out if she knew I was only sixteen, so I kept my mouth closed on the subject of age. Trying to take some of the onus off of myself, I pointed to the table. "That's Kim, my roommate." I raised a corner of my lip and scrunched my nose and watched Kim use the book to cover his face. I guess I was on my own here with the ladies.

"I'm sorry we tricked you with the books." Dee's tone was sincere. "We thought it would be funny."

Here's my chance to change my image. "I thought it was cool," I lied with confidence. "I mean, a little weird at first, sure . . . but I know ghosts aren't real.

"Are you sure about that?" Angel asked with a raised brow.

"Yeah, I'm pretty sure."

"Then why were you in this section?" Angel asked.

"Kim was looking for something." I smiled, thrilled that they bought my lie. "I was just killing time."

The girls smiled back. "Well, I'm glad you're doing better," Dee said.

Angel's eyes darted to her watch. "We have to run. See you around, Gerald," she said as she started toward the exit.

Dee twisted a strand of hair around her finger and twirled it slowly, then threw in a bit of a curtsy and nod. "It was a pleasure meeting you. Hope to see you around." She smiled at me. "Oh, Kim, it was nice to meet you too." I heard her say as she strolled past his table. Their giggles faded away as they headed down the stairs.

I leaned back in my chair and let out a gush of air. "They're gone."

The book lowered, and Kim's eyes appeared. I guess he wanted to make sure I wasn't lying, then he smiled. "We talked to girls."

"No, you didn't. I did, you dork." We both beamed with pride and shared a good laugh.

CHAPTER THREE

Hunger set in, so Kim and I decided to check out The Nest. What an appropriate name for the student center that also contained the dining hall. My mind flashed to Dee as I wondered if something was happening between us. I never paid much attention to the ladies before. Maybe I was more of a man than I thought. *Oh, who am I kidding?*

We walked out of the Nelson Center and past the Pryor Center, home of the literary arts. A large group of students lined the half walls that surrounded The Nest. No one appeared to be waiting in line to eat, so Kim and I walked past and through the double doors.

I was so busy thinking about the possibility of meeting Dee that I had forgotten about the boys wearing black shirts. Three of them were perched near the entrance, and I turned my head to look away. With a little luck, maybe they wouldn't recognize me. I breathed a sigh of relief as we strode past with no confrontation.

The food looked impressive, though maybe that was because it was the first day of college. I noticed several items I wanted to try, and I settled for two slices of pepperoni pizza and a bowl of chocolate pudding. Mom only allowed me to have chocolate pudding on special occasions, like birthdays or holidays, so this was a real treat. I followed Kim as we each grabbed a nice tall glass of Pepsi. Freedom flowed through my veins as I walked with confidence to the rear of the dining hall.

I noticed a couple of guys sitting at a table in the back of the cafeteria and began to make my way toward them. I could feel my nerves twist up my gut as I imagined introducing myself, but I didn't want to be the worm anymore . . . no, not here. I skirted around a few tables and weaved around some students, awkwardly trying not to draw attention to myself. I could tell right away they were like Kim and me from the way they were dressed. It was that plain, boring geek look that I understood too well. One boy hid behind the "Lord of Light." I had heard about that book, but Mom didn't like me reading science fiction. Kim laid his tray on the table and pulled out a chair, and I did the same without saying a word. One of the boy's index finger rose to his face so he could nudge his glasses up to get a better look. A faint smile crossed his face. I knew that look, the one when you're glad it's not the school bully. Why are people so mean to one another? I've never understood that because we're all the same on the inside.

"Hi, I'm Gerald, and this is Kim." I pointed.

"Welcome. I'm Gannon Clark, and this is Desmond Hanks. We went to high school together." Desmond rose his hand and shot us a quick wave. I guess the book he was reading was more important than we were.

Yep, this was my crowd—saying awkward things and reading books at the dinner table. Another tray plopped down beside me, which startled me at first, but I contained my emotions when I noticed it was a girl. Her plate included a salad, along with a glass of water. I looked up as she took her seat. Her hair was dirty blonde, and she wore two ponytails. Her large, black-framed coke-bottle glasses made me think of my Aunt Bertha. Mom's sister was the fun one in the family.

I liked staying with her on the weekends, which was only when my mom would allow. Her straightforward style of clothes reminded me of my wardrobe.

She nodded, and I shot her a wry smile in return. "That's Sandy, Sandy Beach Finlay," Gannon said. "She's a sophomore."

She frowned. "Do you have to tell everyone my middle name?"

"Sorry," Gannon replied with a shrug.

"I think it's pretty cool." I smiled. "Beach."

"Great, then you can have it." She half-smiled and plunged her fork into the salad.

The five of us enjoyed our dinner with minimal conversation. First-day jitters, I guess. Kim rose to take his tray to the return window, and moments later, I heard plates, silverware, and a glass shatter on the floor. Startled, I looked up and saw Kim wasn't moving. He was surrounded by three boys wearing black T-shirts. The room fell silent, and all eyes were on Kim. I lunged to my feet and started toward the group. I'm not sure what I was thinking or what I would do when I got there; I guess I was hoping I could reason with them.

The tallest of the boys seemed agitated as he turned to greet me. "Can I help you?"

"No. Ah, not really," I stuttered as I found a little courage. "I came to help Kim clean up his mess. He's clumsy like that." My heart raced as I bent over and fumbled to pick up the mess on the floor while Kim watched.

"Leave it," the boy demanded. I ignored him and placed the last of the items on the tray. *I didn't want to be the worm or the coward anymore.* I wrapped my hands around the tray and rose to my feet. *Was I being brave or stupid for trying to help someone I met only an hour ago?* Suddenly, the tray sprang from my hands, lunging into the air a few feet. I didn't flinch. It was time to take a stand. I'd been bullied all my life, and it had to stop here and now.

"Does that make you feel masculine?" I looked him in the eye. He gazed back, and I thought he was about to pounce. "Didn't you understand the question?" I managed to get out.

"I understood the question, but I didn't do anything." He looked stunned. "I came over to help him."

"He didn't do it," Kim said quietly.

I stepped back and gazed at Kim. "Trays can't flip themselves."

"It did. It just flew up in the air."

I grappled with what Kim was trying to tell me. "That's impossible," I whispered, my voice sounded raspy.

"Stop it."

I recognized the voice.

"Sam, Gabe, Donnie, stop it," she demanded. "How childish can you be?"

The boys cringed a little. "Babe, I didn't do anything," Sam replied.

“Don’t call me babe when you are acting like a child.” Angel crossed her arms and stood firm. “I thought you were a man . . .” She paused. “Just go.”

“You gotta believe me, I didn’t do anything!” He reached to touch her arm, but she jerked away.

Donnie turned to Sam and tugged his arm. “Let’s go, man.”

“It’s not worth it, man.” Gabe turned for the door. Sam hesitated a little, but Donnie convinced him to leave the hall.

Angel turned to me. “Sorry for their behavior.”

“It’s not your fault, but thanks for sticking up for us.”

“They didn’t do anything,” Kim repeated. “The tray flipped on its own.”

Angel and I turned to face Kim. I knew the minute I looked into his eyes that he was telling the truth. It was one of those gifts I had. I think Angel believed him, too. I noticed Dee had trailed behind the boys. I can’t believe I didn’t see her when we came in. Had she been sitting at the table with Angel when all this started?

“Thanks for your help, Angel.”

She shot me a crooked smile and made her way to join the others. That’s when it hit me. Dee and Angel were both wearing blue jeans and black T-shirts. Were the five of them together? I wanted to run after them and ask, but I decided that might not be the best idea.

I noticed Gannon had come over to wipe the floor with some napkins. I thought he and I were going to get along just fine. “I like the way you stood up to those boys,” Gannon said.

“It was nothing.”

“They didn’t do anything,” Kim chimed in. “You need to listen to me. Those boys didn’t touch my tray, and they didn’t flip the tray when you were holding it, either.”

I blinked a few times. “Do you hear yourself?”

“Listen to me,” he demanded. “I was walking over to place my tray in the return window. I noticed Donnie and his crew walk toward me. I got a little nervous, so I hurried my pace, and then the tray shot straight up in the air.” He took a deep breath. “I’m not sure what happened. Maybe I lost my balance . . . But Donnie and his friends were a few feet away when I dropped my tray. I swear they didn’t touch it.” Kim glanced at me, then to Gannon.

Wow, I’d only known Kim for the better part of the day, but this was the most I’d heard him talk. I giggled on the inside. But the facts bothered me because he wasn’t making sense. I mean, why would he stick up for Donnie? Weren’t Donnie and his friend’s bullies? Could I be jumping to conclusions about them? I didn’t even know these guys; for all I knew, they could be super friendly. “I’m not sure what to say . . . Trays don’t fly by themselves,” I finally responded. I wanted to believe Kim, but I’m a guy who believes in science. *There had to be a logical answer.*

“Why don’t we all go back to the table?” Gannon murmured as he headed in that direction.

I nodded and followed behind. "Wait . . . where's Sandy?"

"She took off." Desmond frowned. I pulled out my chair and nestled in. Gannon sat on the opposite side of the table, and I watched as Kim placed his tray in the return bin. Much to our surprise, he walked toward the door instead of coming back to the table. I leaped to my feet as did Gannon.

"Nice to meet you." I waved to Desmond, then went after Kim. My mother had taught me to be polite, and I didn't want to appear rude in front of my new friends.

I pushed the exit door open, making my way out into the large courtyard surrounding The Nest. Students sat on the half-block walls that lined the walkways. Behind them were large grassy areas surrounded by all sorts of trees. Some students were spread out on blankets, playing cards, reading books, studying, or hanging out. This was nothing like high school. It was a lovely crisp fall evening, great for being outside. I even noticed a few fireflies flickering about. The scene was surreal, and I almost forgot why I'd come out. My eyes scanned to the left, then to the right. There he was, sitting by himself at the end of the wall. Gannon and I made our way over.

"Why'd you leave?"

"Leave me alone," Kim snapped.

"I'm sorry I didn't believe you, it's just hard to swallow, you know?" Things were happening that didn't make sense.

Kim looked up. "Something strange happened that I can't explain. My grandma believes in the supernatural. She says ghosts are everywhere. I don't know because I've never seen one in person, but she has, and she would not lie to me." His demeanor remained steady as his gaze flicked to the ground. "I know what happened today."

I plopped down next to Kim and placed my hand on his shoulder. "We'll figure this out, I promise." I was confident. Maybe it was a magnetic energy field or matter of some kind. Or perhaps someone was pulling a sophisticated gag on a couple of first-year students. That seemed like the logical answer. I would leave no stone unturned until I could prove what really happened in the cafeteria.

Gannon took a spot on the other side of Kim, and we watched as students bustled about the courtyard in singles, pairs, larger groups, boys, and girls. We sat in amazement and people-watched as the evening slipped away. The crowds thinned out over time until the streetlights glared across the empty yard. I looked at my watch and noticed it was already a quarter till eleven.

I yawned. "I think I'm heading back to the dorm. Anyone else coming?" It was my subtle way of letting them know I was tired.

It had nothing to do with being past my bedtime.

CHAPTER FOUR

Morning came quickly. I sprang from my bed, grabbed a quick shower, brushed my teeth, and slipped on my clothes. I grabbed the envelope my mother left me and pulled out a few pages. My eyes darted back and forth as I memorized my class schedule.

I nudged Kim, who remained in bed because his first class was later in the morning than mine. I snatched up my backpack and went out the door, my excitement level soaring to new heights. I was only sixteen, and this was my first day of college. So far, I had managed to keep my age a secret, and I planned to keep it that way. I started down the hall as another door pushed open. Gannon came out wearing a thick plaid sweater with a pair of khaki-colored pants—something my mother would have picked out for me. Today I chose to wear dark blue dress slacks with a light blue button-down long sleeve shirt. I wanted to make a good impression on my first day.

It was so nice to see a friendly face. “Hey, good morning.”

He smiled back. “Where are you heading?”

“I was going to grab a quick breakfast, then head over to Mason Hall. How about you?”

“Same here. I have chemistry at eight-thirty.”

“Me, too.” I smiled. Chemistry, in a nutshell, was a creative discipline chiefly concerned with atomic and molecular structure, and it changes through chemical reactions. Not to mention, it was one of my favorite topics.

"What do you make of Kim's story last night?" Gannon asked.

I was a bit disappointed that Gannon wanted to talk about the mysterious events from last night instead of chemistry or physics. I'm not sure what there was to talk about, so I decided to entertain the idea rather than upset or ignore my new friend. "What do you mean?"

"Well, you've known Kim longer than me. I don't understand why he would make up such a story, do you?"

"You understand I only met Kim an hour before you did?" I gave him a wide-eyed stare.

Gannon lifted his eyebrows in surprise. "Oh, I thought you guys were friends from high school."

"No." I wanted to give more than just a one-word answer, but I wasn't sure what else to add.

Gannon's eyes bored into mine, and he stood unblinking as I shuffled on my feet. I guess he thought I was going to elaborate, and his stare was a bit creepy. We made our way down the stairs to the lobby. I walked outside, and a shiver raced down my spine. I quickly pulled my collar up and shoved my hands into my pockets. I immediately wished I had grabbed a jacket. I noticed Gannon was still waiting for me to respond. "What more do you want me to say?" I snarled.

"Did you see, oh . . . what's his name?" He hesitated. "Donnie, yes, Donnie. Did you see him hit Kim's tray?"

I thought about last night, remembering all the details as they unfolded. "My head was facing down when I heard the sound of Kim's tray hitting the floor. I didn't see anything. I only assumed it was the boys. Kim said they didn't touch it, and if he's telling the truth, the guys were in the clear." I paused to focus on my own experience. "I was holding the tray when I stood up, and I remember it flying up in the air. I never saw Donnie move his hand, and no one's that fast unless they're a superhero. And the other boys were standing behind Donnie, so they couldn't have done it. Science is telling me that they didn't do it. But then, who did?" I whispered loud enough for Gannon to hear, but no one else. I didn't need some random student eavesdropping on my conversation. I didn't want to sound crazy.

We walked toward The Nest in silence. Students lined the block walls of the courtyard, some eating breakfast outside, while others watched or chatted. I didn't realize how hungry I was until the moment we walked through the doors. I was met by the unmistakable, familiar aromas of bacon, eggs, and French toast. This place was better than home. I grabbed my tray and looked up and down the line at all the food we could choose. Mom would want me to take the Corn Flakes and not add sugar, but there was so much to choose from. I placed my plastic tray on the rails and slid down the line. Gannon picked up a fruit cup and two boxes of Frosted Flakes and a glass of milk. I pointed at the scrambled eggs and looked over my shoulder toward the door. I don't know who I was looking for; I guess maybe I was worried Mom would find out. I turned and watched as the lady behind the counter buried the scoop into the eggs and slammed them onto my plate. She moved the tongs into place and latched on to a few strips of bacon and nestled them beside the eggs. I moved on, grabbing two slices of toast, and finished with a tall glass of milk. I firmly gripped my tray—I didn't need any more accidents, especially not with my delicious breakfast. I looked in all directions, aware of my surroundings. I followed Gannon to the table where we sat the night before. I was surprised to see Sandy sitting alone, hiding behind a book.

"Good morning." I smiled, thinking how nice it was to see her again.

Her eyes peeked over the top of the book. "Hey." And a slight nod was all we were going to get out of her. I noticed the book cover, with a cowboy and a girl intertwined. *No, not a romance book.* I shivered at the thought. Maybe it was my age.

I sprinkled salt and pepper on my eggs and then picked up the ketchup bottle and blasted it all over the top. I'm not sure if that's a Pennsylvania tradition. I just know I love ketchup on my eggs; to be honest, everything tastes better with ketchup. It didn't take long to polish off my plate.

"So, we were talking about the flying trays," Gannon said.

Ugh, he's not going to let this go. I thought we were done talking about this. The fact is, I had no answer, which bothered me, and obviously, it was troubling Gannon, too. "I don't know what happened last night," I chirped, my speech reverting to my younger years. I thought my voice change had ended. I guess I thought wrong on that subject, too.

"There has to be an explanation."

I looked at Gannon. "What you're saying couldn't have happened. It defies the law of physics. Objects don't move by themselves, and trays don't fly out of people's hands.

Someone had to hit the tray for it to move. End of discussion." I knew I was right. I had to be.

"Excuse me, can I add something?" My eyes flew wide as did Gannon's, when Sandy decided to chime in on our conversation. Maybe we were about to get our butts chewed for talking while she was trying to read, and my mouth hung open with anticipation.

"I'm sorry," Gannon replied. I nodded to let her know I was sorry, too.

"I finished my dinner last night. I watched as the Asian boy stood and walked toward the tray return area—"

"His name's Kim Lu." I smirked and noticed how flush Gannon's face was as his eyes bored into mine for the second time this morning.

"May I continue?" she spat back.

"Please do." I waved a hand to let her know the floor was hers.

"Kim Lu," she said slowly and gritted her teeth at me, "made his way to the return area. Three other boys approached." Gannon turned to me and gave me this look that told me to keep my mouth shut, which I did, but for the record, his name was Donnie. "They were a few feet away when they stopped. Something was blocking them from getting too close to Kim. It blinked white and was gone at the same time the tray flew up in the air."

"What blinked white?" I asked, confused.

"It appeared to be translucent, but it took the shape of a person. Then it was gone." Gannon's eyes crossed and blinked at me a few times. I think we were both confused. "That's when you stood up. Oh, do I need to use your name, too?" Her eyes bulged at me. "You walked over to Kim. I wasn't sure what your intentions were. Then you bent over and helped clean up the mess. I watched to see what would happen next, and as you stood, the clear thing showed up, and I noticed an upward flash, and then the tray was launched skyward."

I couldn't be hearing this correctly. Everyone knows ghosts don't exist. "Wait one minute. Are you saying you saw a ghost?" I cocked my head and gave her a sideways look.

"Yes, that is exactly what I'm saying. At first, I thought I was crazy, but I know I'm not. That's why I left so abruptly. I went over this a hundred times in my head. I know what I witnessed. It was something like a ghostly figure." She gazed at me and then at Gannon. I'm good at reading people and I knew she was being honest—this wasn't some prank.

Gannon glanced at his wristwatch. "Class is about to start." He stood, grabbed his tray, and marched to the bin. I grabbed my backpack, slung it over my shoulder, and then grabbed my tray and followed.

"I'm not crazy. I know what I saw," Sandy hollered as we walked away.

I didn't want to be late on the first day, so I kept walking and didn't look back. Her story was puzzling. Why would someone make up a story like that? By the look on her face, she was telling the truth. These thoughts would have to wait. I picked up my pace, almost to a light jog, to keep up with

Gannon. Down the sidewalk, around the corner, and Mason Hall came into view.

Gannon was almost at a full sprint, and I started to run, too. Others stared at us as they sauntered in the same direction. We burst through the front door, the classroom was to our left, and I noticed the door was still open, which was a good sign. I was taken aback as we entered the large room. It was like walking into a small auditorium, with only about a hundred seats. Many were empty, and I started my descent down the stairs. Gannon and I must have shared the same thought because he headed for the front row, too. I always like the front row because hearing and visibility were excellent. We found two seats in the front row, right in the middle. Today was our lucky day.

Minutes passed, and Gannon looked at his watch every thirty seconds. I watched more students pour into the class. No bell? No teacher? Were we in the right place? My heart rate accelerated. I couldn't fathom the thought that we may be in the wrong classroom. I was about to have a panic attack when the rear doors began to close. A side door opened, and a tall, stout fellow walked in carrying a brown-leather briefcase. I watched as he slid it under the podium, and then laid a few papers in front of him and looked from side to side. His face was slightly wrinkled, with a touch of gray hair in his sideburns. He wore brown corduroy pants and a light brown plaid shirt with a neat little bow tie. He appeared to be the typical professor I had envisioned in my mind.

"Welcome to freshman chemistry." His voice was raspy. "I'm Professor Ream, yes, just like a ream of paper." His voice rose. "I don't like paper jokes, so if you want to get on my bad side, that's a quick way to do it."

I raised my hand—*look at me, the first student to have a question.* Professor Ream cocked his head and gazed at me. "Yes, the student in the front row."

I eased my hand down. "I didn't hear a bell to signify the start of class."

"And you are?" he asked slowly, then glanced at the papers before him.

"I'm Gerald."

He fumbled through the pages, "Oh, so you're Gerald Dupickle, my fifteen-year-old prodigy child." He looked up at me as I heard chuckles scatter around the room. I tried to push myself down in the seat with the hopes no one would remember me, but it was too late. My secret was out. Everyone on campus was going to know my name and age before the day was over.

I'm not sure why, but I felt the need to correct him. "I'm sixteen."

"I'm sorry," his eyes drilled through me, "*sixteen-year-old* Gerald, let me make one thing clear, this is not high school. There are no bells. I'm sure you all own a watch and know how to tell time, so be here on time if you want to learn. The class starts when I walk in the door. I don't care if you're late. You get out of college what you put into it. After all, it's your parents' money you're wasting, not mine. I get paid the same. If you want to sleep, then stay home. If you want to skip class, that's fine. As long as you do the homework and pass the exams, I will pass you. There is no roll call in college. Are we clear?"

“Yes, sure, ah-ha,” were mumbled around the room. I just nodded and watched Gannon frown at me.

“Now, if I may continue, welcome to freshman chemistry. We have a busy semester ahead of us, and I plan to throw a lot at you.” This time, I kept my mouth shut. I think I was too scared to ask any more questions. I sat quietly, took notes, and listened to what Professor Ream had to say. In the blink of an eye, the class was over.

“I need you to think about a few things this week,” Ream said. “Why are you here? Are you here to kill time? Or are you here to change time?” He paused. “Dismissed.” I watched as he stuffed the papers into his case and walked out the door. I shoved my notebook inside my backpack and followed Gannon out to the hall. The professor’s question lingered in my mind.

CHAPTER FIVE

Today's class didn't go as I had expected. I wondered how fast word would spread about my name and age. Would they remember if I was fifteen or sixteen? And would the pickle head jokes come out in full force? Gannon plopped down on the half wall outside in the courtyard and I did the same.

"You okay?" he asked.

"Yeah, I'm fine, just embarrassed." I sat, bouncing my feet off the wall as I stared at the ground.

"Why? You don't look like you're sixteen."

"Thanks, but today I felt like a kid again." I frowned.

"How would you have known? I mean, I was wondering if they sound the bells for the class to start, too."

"Yeah, but you didn't ask the question . . . I did."

"Hello, boys."

My head snapped to attention. "Hi, Dee." I smiled and gave a short wave. "Hi, Angel."

"Who's this?" Angel asked.

"This is Gannon,"

"Hi, ladies," Gannon replied.

"This is Dee and Angel." I pointed.

"Nice to meet you, Gannon." Angel smiled.

"How was your first class?" Dee asked.

"Not quite what I had expected after the professor reamed me a new one." I got a chuckle out of Gannon.

"Don't let little things bother you, Gerald. That's the best advice I can give you," Angel offered.

"Hey, we're having a small gathering this evening. Would you two like to come?" Dee asked. "It's at Fang's place."

"Ah, um . . . I don't know." I paused to look at Gannon. His eyes were wide and mouth agape. "Ah, maybe another time. I need to study," I apologized. I wasn't sure where Fang's place was—I assumed it was a college food spot or hangout. *I want to get to know Dee, though. She seems nice, but I haven't hung out with many girls and figure maybe I should do a little research first. Was she dating one of the other guys? Or did she like me?* The suspicious side of me took over, and my gut was screaming, *It's a trap!*

"Gannon, can you make it?" Dee swayed back and forth.

"Nah, I have homework, sorry."

"That's fine, school first, I understand." She smiled like everything was okay, but I detected a hint of disappointment in her voice.

"See you around, boys." I watched as Angel and Dee moved across the courtyard. Dee paused once to look over her shoulder, and I caught a glimpse of her smile.

The minute they were out of earshot, I blurted out, "Where's Fang's place?"

"How would I know? I'm a freshman, too." Gannon shook his head. "Hey, did you realize Angel remembered your name? That's a good sign." He smiled.

"It means nothing, anyway. I kind of like Dee, though. She's cute." We dismissed the idea and both enjoyed another laugh.

Over the next few hours, we studied, shared notes, and even worked on some of the early readings that were assigned. Before long, it was lunch, so we made our way over to The Nest and grabbed a quick bite. I pulled out my books and began to study a little more. Another lucky break, Gannon and I had the same afternoon class, freshman math.

I survived the first day of college. After dinner, Gannon went back to the dorm, but I decided to stroll over to the library. I found the book I needed and decided to go to the third floor to study. How busy could the paranormal section be? Just as I thought, the room was empty. I pushed my way to the back, found an isolated table, plopped down, and began to read advanced chemistry.

The hours passed, and my head popped up when I thought I heard something like a hint of laughter. *My mind must be playing tricks on me*. I looked around, but I was alone. I continued to read, but there it was again—someone was snickering, a female voice. I gazed around. I was still alone, so I shrugged and dove back into my book. A minute later, I heard a loud plop echo in the empty room. Startled, I jumped, only because it was so quiet, and then, I smiled. The girls must have found me. I decided to ignore them. Minutes passed, and I heard another book hit the floor. I looked up and laid my book on the table. *So, this was how they wanted to play it, huh?* I stood, tiptoed to the first rack, quickly peeked around the corner . . . nothing. Puzzled, my heart began to pound. I tiptoed to the next aisle. I felt giddy, like a kid on Christmas. This was the first time in my life that I had a girl interested in me—and I liked it.

I snapped my head around the next corner, still nothing. It had to be Dee. Okay, maybe I was *hoping* it was Dee. I wiped my palms on my slacks as I started toward the next row, my heart beating faster with every step. I quickly stopped and peered down the long row of books. I noticed a book shaking on the shelf. *Books don't quiver. How odd.* The book started to slide out about half an inch, and I gasped. It paused and then moved again. I knew the girls must be enjoying themselves, thinking they could trick me twice. I'm too smart for that, but I can let them think were fooling me. The book jerked forward and teetered a little, then finally toppled to the floor. I lunged forward to the next row. "Got you!" Much to my surprise, the row was empty. And they didn't have time to escape since I was too close.

I looked around in all directions. The place was empty, I was sure of it. I looked back down the row at the three books lying on the floor. I cautiously made my way down the aisle. I stepped forward, my pulse racing, looked over my shoulder, then forward again. Another step. *Where were they?* I wiped my palms against my slacks as I looked behind, then forward. I repeated my actions until I was standing over the book. Something felt wrong. I took one last glance down the aisle and then over my shoulder again. I knelt and turned the book over. "Do You Believe in Ghosts?" That was the same book that Dee and Angel had pushed out. How could that be? I shook it off. I guess the girls knew what books to push.

I felt a sharp pain as something slapped me in the back of the head. I bounced back and placed my hand over the divot in my head. I rubbed it briefly. Then I noticed a fourth book lying on the floor. *Hardcover books hurt more than paperbacks*. I bent over and flipped the book around. "Proof that Ghosts Exist." My memory's excellent, so I know without a shadow of a doubt that this was the second book the girls had pushed off the shelves. My hand jolted forward, and I tossed the next book over, "How to Catch a Ghost." Three for three. This is crazy or impossible. One more book was lying on the floor. Why were they all landing face down? What are the odds of that? I wish Gannon were here to see this. I knew it had to be the girls, or if not, then maybe Donnie, Gabe, or the other boy Sam.

I turned the last book over. "True Ghost Stories." I don't think they're real. Ghosts are only fiction, nothing more; it's never been proven. I straightened up and glanced down the row. I sprinted to the end of the aisle before jumping around the corner. No one was there. I dashed from row to row, ready to pull my hair out. I went back and forth, but the floor was empty, no one, only me. I must have looked like a madman running back and forth. I couldn't understand; things didn't add up. *One and one is two. Two and two, four. I must be losing my mind—maybe a small bout of madness since this is my first time away from home*. I sprinted to the other end of the room. Nothing. Back to the front, I darted. Still, no one. No matter which way I went, it was apparent that I was the only person on the third floor. How was that possible?

I scrambled over to the stairs, turned, and gazed back over the vacant floor. I turned around, facing the stairs, and observed the floors below over the balcony railing. I could see students on the first floor, coming up the staircase, and stopping on the second floor. I received a few weird looks as people made their way past the third floor. I scurried up behind the last group of kids and stopped on the fourth floor. Students galore. What the heck? The place was busy, yet nobody was staying on the third floor. I placed my hands on the back of my head, scrunched my fingers, and pulled my hair. *It's true . . . I've done lost my mind.*

Deep breaths, inhale, exhale, I repeated to myself. "You okay, dude?" A guy stopped to check on me. I nodded yes, so he moved on. My breathing slowed. I gradually started my descent to the third floor but paused in the stairwell. I even took a few steps to overlook the second floor again. Yes, every level had students rummaging about. Now my interest was piqued. Why didn't anyone go to the third floor? Had I missed something in freshman orientation? I shuffled my feet and ended up standing on the threshold, overlooking the deserted level of the library.

I read the signs to all the different sections—Cooking, Travel, Foreign, and Paranormal, all titles no college student would be interested in reading, in my opinion. Why was such a large part dedicated to ghosts, ghouls, and spirits? Had there been that many books written about ghosts? I was amazed. I had no idea. I glanced down the first row—ghost hunting, how to find a ghost? The next row—how to hold a séance. Wow, I had no clue. I peeked down the next few rows and noticed many sections were empty.

I paused, staring down the walkway. The books were gone . . . What? I tugged at my hair and scanned the section. I was alone, so how could this be? I'm losing my mind. It has to be something I ate—probably should have stuck with the sensible Corn Flakes like Mom would have said. Was I missing home? I marched down the aisle and hovered where the books once were, but they were back where they belonged. It defied the law of physics. I looked forward then back.

Something flickered out of the corner of my eye. I froze, then raised my head slightly and gazed down at the other end of the shelves. A small set of lights appeared and began to twinkle in a circular motion. I blinked. What was I seeing? A book was suspended in midair. That's impossible. I straightened up and noticed the spine on the book. I whispered out loud as I read the title, "How to Catch a Ghost." I grabbed the book and turned it over in my hands. I looked up and the lights grew brighter, more abundant, transforming into a white mass. "I-is anyone h-here?" I stuttered as loud as my wary voice would allow.

At that moment, I was feeling much like the worm who was about to be devoured. I'm not sure why, but that summer day still haunted me. "This isn't funny," I whimpered. I felt frozen in place. I must be stressing out—new school jitters and tired because I was up later than I should have been. That has to be it. I didn't know what to do.

Here I was, face to face with something I couldn't explain, something that logically couldn't exist, yet I was witnessing this with my own eyes. "I must be dreaming," I said as I started to laugh. Mom was right, I needed to go to bed earlier. I chuckled louder and rapidly brought my hand toward my face until I felt the sharp pain of impact. Now I wanted to cry. I was wide awake, this was real, and the thing at the end of the row was growing in size and brightness, manifesting into the shape of a small human. At least, I think it's human, but what if it's an alien? A being who traveled from a faraway galaxy to meet someone as intelligent as me? Someone who could understand. I was honored to be chosen. I briefly smiled, then had another thought, *I've seen a few space movies. Nothing good ever comes from aliens landing on Earth.*

Panic deepened my senses. I needed to move, run, get out of there. But my backpack was lying on the table in the rear of the room. *Okay*, I quickly thought up a plan. *I'll take one step back at a time and put some distance between me and whatever this thing is*. I stumbled back one step. The translucent mass drifted closer. I moved my other foot back and the object followed me. This wasn't working. I felt light-headed, dizzy. I grasped the edge of the bookshelf with my right hand to balance. I took a few deep breaths and closed my eyes. When I reopened them, I was hoping the large white mass would be gone—like a hallucination would be. Instead, it was standing before me.

I shivered and noticed that it felt colder than it had a few moments ago. I was a man—okay, a boy—who believed in science, things that needed to be proven by testing. So why was I having a hard time understanding what I was seeing? Okay, let me correct myself . . . *floating* before me was an alien, a real-life alien. I exhaled. I knew what I needed to do. *Be brave*. "Hello," I squeaked. *Hello?* Was that the best I could do? I'm the first person on this planet to talk with someone from another world or possibly even a ghost, and all I could say was hello?

I swallowed hard and tried again. "Hi, I'm Gerald." I pointed a finger to my chest. "Who are you?" I pointed at the mass and waited for a response. The mass in front of me took a different appearance. It was a girl, and she looked human. I could see her, yet through her. She was wearing a white, floor-length dress, slightly ripped on the right side. She had curly hair trickling down the sides of her face. She looked puzzled, frightened for some reason. I was the one who should be scared. "Can you talk?" She tilted her head to one side. I think she was as surprised as I was that I could see her. "Are you alright?" I managed to ask. She pulled back a little and looked me up and down.

Her neck looked a little funny . . . kind of crooked. "Can you hear me?" She floated upward a foot or two, making herself appear larger. "I'm not going to hurt you." I don't know why I said that. I wouldn't even know how to hurt an alien or ghost. I mention alien again because I didn't know what this thing—person, being—standing before me was. *Could it be a ghost?* I extended my hand in her direction and slightly waved. My eyes widened with excitement as she raised her hand to meet mine. My breath fluttered and my mouth hung open. I was on the verge of a giant breakthrough in the name of science. Her hand hovered a few inches away from mine. Her entire body blinked in and out for a few moments. "Are you alright?" I asked her again. I wondered if she could hear me or understand what I was saying. How could I uncover the secrets to our universe if I couldn't communicate?

"Do you understand me?" I pointed to myself again. "Who are you? Do you have a name?" I asked as my heart thumped in my chest. Why wouldn't she answer me? I needed answers. "Where are you from?" I paused. "What planet do you come from?" I waited for her to answer. "Are you an alien?" I grew with excitement. I was hoping for a yes, but she cracked a quick smile, almost a laugh. So, I took that as a no, she was not alien. Dang it, I was hoping to be the first human to meet an extraterrestrial being. She opened her mouth. She was going to say something, but then she got startled and closed it quickly.

Footsteps, snickering, and laughter approached from the rear. Someone was coming. Oh, my goodness, I hoped they could see her, too then I would have the proof I needed. People would believe me if there were two or more witnesses. I looked over my shoulder, then back to her. She appeared frightened and started to back away. "Don't go," I whispered. "Please don't leave." But she pulled away as the voices grew louder as they approached. I looked over my shoulder once more, hoping whoever was about to arrive would catch a glimpse of her.

I stepped in her direction, but before any words could leave my mouth, she bolted directly through me. A cold chill pierced me like a razor blade. I felt paralyzed. My life flashed before my eyes. I was a kid again, sitting on the front porch with my mother enjoying sandwiches and chips and a tall glass of Kool-Aid in the summer breeze. The cold chill hardened every bone in my body. I could feel myself topple. I was falling backward in slow motion. There was nothing I could do.

Pain riveted through my entire body when the back of my head bounced off the hardwood floor. My fingers opened, and I felt the book spiral out of reach. I heard voices, boys and girls, and footsteps closing in. The room spun as I closed my eyes. The sting of the impact lingered, and the air oozed out of my lungs.

CHAPTER SIX

The world looked dark and empty; time froze, then righted itself. I heard whispers in the distance. "Gerald?" It sounded like a male voice. "Is he alive?" a female asked. I could feel light taps against my cheeks, yet I could not move. I was paralyzed. The room clouded over. Maybe I had lost my vision. Everything was off. Voices faded in and out. I could hear, feel, and speak, but no one heard me or noticed I was alive. *Is this death?* I tried to blink. I caught a glimpse of light. It flickered for a moment. Another tap on my cheek, and I stirred. "He's alive." Her voice sounded familiar.

"Roll him over," the man instructed.

"Wait, what if he's hurt?" another voice chimed in. "Don't move him."

I tried to remember. *Yes, books falling off the shelves. A girl appeared. Was I talking to an alien? A female from another world? She must have stunned me with a futuristic laser gun . . . But how awesome is that? I'd be the first human to be shot and survive an alien attack.*

My eyes blinked open, and everything was blurred. I noticed a small crowd gathered around me. Startled, they jumped back when my lips moved. "I'm fine," I slurred, my tongue heavy and useless. I noticed Donnie hovering over me—I recognized his curly blonde hair, which matched mine, though I'd never noticed before. He was still wearing a black T-shirt. *Does he own any other color?* To his right, I spotted Gabe with his black crew cut, and behind him, Sam, who was a bit taller, but sported the same style hair as Gabe. Then I noticed a tall fellow that I didn't recognize. I smiled at the sight of Angel, and behind her, Dee.

"He's alive!" the guy in the back row called out as he pushed his way to the front. "I'm Fang, and you must be Gerald?" My eyes focused and I tried to talk, but my mouth felt numb like I'd had a shot of Novocain. My cheek felt wet. *Oh crap, I'm drooling on myself!* I rolled to my side to hide my face from Dee and Angel.

"Easy, big guy." Donnie lowered his hand to stop me from moving. "It's okay, you're going to be alright," Donnie tried to reassure me. He pulled a handkerchief from his pocket and wiped the drool from the side of my face. I nodded in approval.

"Can you tell me what happened?" the tall boy wearing the black Beatles shirt asked. I didn't recognize him; wait, he said his name was Fang. *Who names their kid Fang? Is that what Dee meant when she said they were going to Fang's place?* Fang sported a bit of facial hair, and he stood taller and more confident in his skin. The others moved out of the way for him and let him take over, almost as if he was their leader.

I tried to sit up. Lightheaded, I started to fall backward. Fang cupped his hand under my head and gently laid me to the floor. "Grab a few books," he insisted.

I felt something hard slide under my feet. "Let's see if that helps get some blood back in your face."

The minutes passed, and I started to feel better, and finally, I was able to sit up. Then Donnie and Fang each placed a hand under my armpit and hoisted me to my feet.

Bracing myself with my arms over Donnie and Fang's shoulders, we hiked to the nearest table. Gabe pulled out a chair and helped guide me. My body felt drained as I took my seat. Fang pulled out another chair and sat before me. "Gabe, he needs water." Gabe darted off in a flurry while the others pulled out chairs and took spots around me.

"How are you feeling, Gerald?" Concern resonated in Fang's voice.

"I'm tired, and my mouth's dry."

"Gabe's getting you some water." He paused and looked over his shoulder. "Can you tell me what happened?"

"Books."

He scowled. "Books?"

"The books fell."

"Falling books . . ." Fang appeared confused.

I mustered the words he needed to hear. "The books started falling off the shelf."

Gabe darted over and pushed his way through before shoving a tall cup of water at Fang. Fang extended his hand, grabbed the container, and tilted the cup to my lips. Oh, that felt good. It was cold and refreshing.

"Thanks."

"You said the books started falling off the shelf."

"Yes, the books fell on the floor, then they were back on the shelf, and one floated toward me. That's when she appeared."

"We didn't see any girl." He stared the others down. "Did you see anyone?" I watched as they shook their heads. "Sorry, Gerald, we only spotted you. We arrived just in time to see you crash to the floor."

"She shocked me with her hand or hit me with a blast of something." I know I sounded like a lunatic. Considering the circumstances, maybe I was losing my mind. Had I seen her? I tugged with the possibility that I had imagined the entire thing. But why had I passed out? Did I have enough to eat or drink today? That had to be it . . . or had I been studying too hard? Stress could do that to a person.

"Gerald, are you okay, man?" There was a desperate edge to Fang's voice. "I believe you, and we're all here to help." I watched as they all smiled.

"I don't understand . . . Why are you nice?" I paused to catch my breath. "I thought you guys were the campus bullies."

"What gave you that idea? We're not bullies . . . far from it." Fang looked shocked as he swayed back and forth.

"The cafeteria incident." I shrugged. "And when my suitcase crashed open on my first day."

"That was a misunderstanding, nothing more, I promise."

"Really?"

"We mean you no harm, you can trust me." Fang stared at the others and each bowed their heads to acknowledge what he said was true. "So, can you tell us what you saw?"

"Alright." I took a deep breath. "I saw a girl, but . . . I think she was an alien." I paused to see if they were going to laugh, but they didn't. They were intent on hearing everything I had to say. I was surprised, really. I thought they would laugh. "She was wearing a long white dress, but it looked ripped on the right side," I closed my eyes to envision her again and popped them open, "and her head, I mean . . . her neck looked crooked. And she had curly hair trickling down the sides of her face."

Fang's mouth hung open, his eyes wide like he had seen a ghost. I glanced at the others, who all had the same wide-eyed, open-mouthed expression. What had I said? Were they about to laugh? Their silence was killing me. Was this part of a cruel joke?

I studied them before I looked back at Fang. "Did I say something wrong?"

"Not at all." He smiled, and I was relieved when he began to speak. "Twenty years ago, a female college student named Victoria Dennard died on this floor. Legend has it she was wearing a white dress and had curly hair the night she perished. I've seen her picture in an old photo. It sounds like you met her."

I was a little stunned by what Fang was telling me, and I motioned for him to continue.

"They say the third floor is haunted. That's why no one comes to this part of the libr—"

“Are you saying I saw a ghost?” I interrupted. I couldn’t believe he’s insinuating that I met a ghost.

“Yes, I think you have.”

“That’s impossible.” I shook my head and threw my hands up. “I’m pretty sure it was an alien.”

Fang snickered, and some of the others raised eyebrows or turned away as not to laugh in my direction. “I’m saying that you didn’t see an alien; it was Victoria. She resides on this floor.”

“That’s impossible. Ghosts don’t exist.” I smirked.

“But you think aliens do?”

“Well, if this planet has life, then it’s obvious there could be other planets that have living creatures. She could have time jumped to this planet and landed here in the library.”

“You believe in aliens and not ghosts?” Fang asked slowly, and I nodded. “Well, if it’s possible to have aliens, then please keep an open mind and consider the possibilities of ghosts.”

“I guess anything’s possible,” I said reluctantly. It was hopeless and wasn’t worth the argument, even though I liked a good debate. I decided to let him think I believed in ghosts. However, I was a little curious. *How convenient that he and his small gang showed up just as I was talking to an alien or ghost.* “What brings you to the third floor if this place is haunted, hmm?” I smirked.

“I’m glad you asked. I’m Frank Warner, but my friends call me Fang because I have two fangs in my mouth.” He smiled to reveal two long, sharp-looking teeth, one on each side. *He would make an incredible Dracula for Halloween.* "I was born with them, and my parents didn't have the money to have them corrected when I was young. I'm also the president of the local chapter of ghost hunters. Let me properly introduce you to the team. That's Sam, the Sniper. He's good at pinpointing where we should be positioned to track the ghost, and he's always trying to catch one." Sam nodded and waved.

"This is Gabe, the Gabster as we call him. He likes to play practical jokes, but not when we're on-site hunting the super-natural. He's our data collector and owns most of the equipment. His parents have money." Gabe gave me a slight wave. "Then we have Donnie, the Demon Hunter. He's not afraid of anything, and he's always the first one in the door. He'll dive headfirst into a haunted room." Donnie shot me a crazed smile, and I'm not gonna lie, it was kind of creepy.

"Behind Donnie, is Angela Weidman, we call her Angel because she looks out for us and takes care of so many things that I can't name them all. She also has the biggest heart of anyone I've ever met." Frank smiled at her as if he was flirting, and she smiled back and winked. Confusion washed over me at the exchange. I thought Angel and Sam were together? "That takes us to Deidre Rose, but we call her Dee for short. She's the shy one. If you can believe that, she also documents everything we discover and keeps all our records neat and tidy. I don't know what we would do without her." Dee smiled, and her cheeks flushed. "We call them the double-trouble twins. The two of them together can get into a ton of trouble when left alone." Fang smiled.

Huh, they didn't look like twins . . . they didn't look anything like each other.

"That brings us back to you. Tell me a little about yourself."

I sneered because I hate talking about myself. "I'm Gerald Dupickle," I nervously spat out, and I was sure they would burst out laughing. Luckily, they didn't, and I was stunned. *This should floor them.* "I'm sixteen." I smirked and paused as I spotted a few nods, but most remained calm. I was impressed. It seemed like they took me seriously. "I have an I.Q. of 159, one-point shy of being a genius. I pretty much remember everything I read and see." Wow. No jokes were being made. Maybe I was wrong about these guys. "If you haven't figured it out yet, I'm kind of a geek." They peered at me, waiting for me to carry on. "I'm a freshman here at the school." Okay, that sounded dorky. I realized they could figure out I go to school here, yet no one made fun of me. "My father and mother are divorced. My mother raised me. We live in upstate Pennsylvania, and my best friend is Bates Bergan, but I call him Hammer because he's big and hurts people who pick on me."

Fang smiled and extended his hand. "Welcome to the club, Gerald."

"Wait a minute . . . who said I was joining any club?" I gazed at Fang. If my eyes contained lasers, they would have drilled right through his head. *No one tells me what to do, except my mom.*

"Of course, you're going to join the club. You have the magnetism we need." His smile begged me to join. "You have the charm to draw ghosts out. We need that."

"Hold up, what makes you think that?"

"It's obvious. You drew Victoria out; she came to you. She hasn't been seen in almost five years. Every now and then someone comes along who has the gift, and you have that gift!"

"I'm not sure I understand." I shook my head. "I don't have any gifts."

"Trust me, you have a gift. I can see it and feel it. It tugs at me. Welcome to the brotherhood of ghost hunters," Fang said as he shot me another smile bearing those fangs of his. "Are you feeling better? If so, let's get out of here." He pulled on my arm as he helped me to my feet.

"Wait, my bag." I pointed to the table skirting the wall. Gabe was gone in a flash and retrieved my bag. Relief flooded me. I didn't want to lose my homework.

I stood, my legs held firm, with no wobble. I guess I was okay. The gang started for the stairs. Dee approached and locked her arm in mine, and she stilled me with her smile. I followed like a lost puppy. I guess I was in need of a home. For once in my life, people wanted to be around me. I had more than one friend; I had several. The thought occurred to me, w*hat if they are using me? I guess time will tell.* And the way Dee held my arm when we walked, I could only wonder if she was my girlfriend. My stomach twitched at the thought. I didn't know what to say to her. I only smiled. I couldn't wait to write a letter to Bates and let him know about my new friends. He worried about me when I left for college but look at me now. I was part of the popular crowd.

CHAPTER SEVEN

Last night was a bit of a blur. My encounter took a lot out of me. I'm not ready to rule out my alien theory yet. I couldn't shake the fact that Dee seemed to like me, I could tell by the way she looked at me and if I remember, I think she winked at me before the night was over.

I remember going to Fang's place and joining his ghost hunting team. But I'm not sure how I got back to my dorm. Oh wait, Gabe gave me a lift, I remember now.

For the first time in my life, I felt like things were going my way. I fit in, and I even had six new friends. I quickly finished my letter to Bates and stuffed it inside the envelope. I couldn't wait to receive his response. I noticed my roommate was already gone, which seemed odd since he mainly had late morning and afternoon classes. In the meantime, I decided to visit Gannon. I would feel better if he would join the team. Safety in numbers, they say, and I bet he'd be fascinated with the paranormal stuff.

I rapped on his door a few times, then finally heard movement within. The door slowly opened; Gannon stood before me wearing nothing but a bright red pair of boxers. "What do you want?" he barked and rubbed the sleep from his eyes. "Sorry, that didn't come out right. Come in." The door opened wide, and I marched in. Gannon motioned me to the chair, but I was too excited to sit.

"I saw a ghost last night." The words flew out of my mouth as I paced back and forth. I wanted to retract my statement, but it was too late. Gannon stared at me like I was insane, and honestly, I couldn't blame him. That would have been my first reaction.

"What are you talking about?" He turned his back to me and looked around. "I'm glad my roommate's not here." He shook his head and walked to the counter to make a pot of coffee. "Do you realize it's only six a.m.?" Then he turned to face me.

"Sorry, I didn't think about the time," I said, my excitement spewing.

Gannon said nothing. He pulled a paper towel from the roll and wiped out a mug that sat next to the coffeemaker. Then he grabbed a second cup of coffee for me. "Would you like some coffee?" he asked as he poured the first cup.

"No thanks, I'm too hyped as it is. Besides, my mother says I'm too young to drink that stuff."

Gannon shook his head as he poured, then added some sugar. "If you're not going to sit, then I will." He eased his way into the cushioned chair in the corner of the room. He sat with his eyes closed and sniffed the aroma first, then took a sip and sighed. "So, what were you saying about ghosts?"

I told Gannon what had happened the night before—not leaving out any details. He listened intensely, shrugging a shoulder from time to time with an occasional *ah-ha* or *I see*. When I finished, he sat in silence. I even added that Dee might be my girlfriend, but still, he said nothing.

"Well?" The anticipation of his response was driving me crazy. Patience was not one of my strong suits.

“Okay, I’m happy you joined their group, and for you having a girlfriend . . . Are you sure they’re not playing you for a fool?” His voice was one of concern.

“I’m not sure about Dee being my girlfriend, but the rest of it was real.” I went silent and waited for his response, but Gannon just stared at me and nursed his coffee. “So, would you like to go with me to meet them?” I asked awkwardly.

“I’ve already met them, remember?”

“They’re not like you think. I mean, they seem nice and sincere. I swear.”

We sat in silence for the longest time. I thought Gannon was going to nod off, but then he finally answered, though his tone was flat, “Okay, I’ll go with you.”

“Alright, I knew I could count on you.” My excitement level increased another notch. “Let’s go.” I motioned to the door.

“It’s six-twenty in the morning. I’m not going anywhere until later. First, I need a shower, then something to eat. Besides, I have a class at ten-thirty, and then another class this afternoon, so let’s plan for this evening. Sound good?”

I frowned but agreed. It’s not like I had a choice—the big question was, what was I going to do this morning? I only had advanced science today, and it wasn’t until mid-afternoon. I decided to go back to my room and try to get some sleep or finish any homework.

* * *

The day slipped away. After dinner, Gannon and I ventured across campus toward Fang's place. He was quiet for most of the trip. The sun had set, and darkness was fast approaching. I could feel the coolness in the fall air, making me wish I had brought a sweater. We walked several blocks to the edge of the campus property. I hadn't noticed until now that on the back of the university entrance sign was the school motto, *where education comes first, and academics soar high!* Nice tie in since this was the home of the Eagles. The buildings transitioned to large single-family homes. A large white and gold sign hung over the doorway on the first home, Sigma Pi. *Well, that makes sense . . . frat houses.* Garnet and gold colors donned the PI Kappa Alpha house, which was were where the jocks hung out.

On the next block were some of the women's sororities—Chi Omega and Delta Gamma. Farther down the road were a few stores and apartment buildings and a local pizza place, The Snack Shack. The rumor around school was that they served the best hoagies and pizza in town.

I caught a hint of the smell as we passed, and my stomach growled. Ignoring my noisy stomach, I followed the directions Dee gave me. At the next intersection, we turned left down a dark alley. "It's at the end of the street." I waved a hand in that direction.

Gannon acknowledged, and we walked down the narrow alley, only wide enough to allow one car passage. A strange smell lingered in the air—it could be rotten food from the restaurant at the corner of the alley. I hadn't noticed that last night. Something stirred up ahead, and Gannon slowed his pace, and I slowed to match his speed. My eyes darted behind a dumpster, and relief washed over me because it was not a person. The sound came from inside the trash—I didn't want to wait to find out what was inside. In one swift motion, Gannon slammed his hand on the side of the metal container. A few cats leaped up and out over the lid and streaked across the street. I think the cats were as startled as me. Gannon chuckled, and we quickened our pace. Behind the old apartment building was a large rundown home, built around the turn of the century. I'm sure it was once a pristine mansion, but now it served as an apartment building for students. On the left side, stairs had been added to allow access to the second and third floors. I pointed up the stairs. I could see the lights were on, so I was sure Fang was home. We ascended, passing the second floor, and a light flickered. Someone was watching TV. The other apartment was dark. Maybe no one was home.

There was only one residence on the top floor, and it belonged to Fang. Someone had converted the attic into a small apartment. I rapped my knuckles against the door. I watched the knob slowly turn, and the door wedged open. "Hey, Gerald, I'm glad you made it, and you brought a friend," Fang greeted us.

"This is Gannon; he's also a freshman." I squeezed through the opening and pointed behind me.

Gannon waved. "Hi."

Cheers rang out as we walked through the door. Wow, everyone was glad to see me. For once in my life, I was the star of the show. *So, is this what it feels like to be famous*? I noticed Donnie, Angel, and Sam sitting on an old brown couch, though I didn't notice Dee or Gabe. I introduced everyone to Gannon, and I couldn't help but notice he was smiling, too.

"Gabe and Dee will be back in a few minutes. They went to pick up the pizza," Fang announced. "I hope you're hungry!"

"That wouldn't be from the Snack Shack, would it?" Gannon asked.

Donnie grinned. "The one and only."

Even though we already had dinner at the Eagles Nest, I couldn't wait to bite down on a slice of that pizza and see if it lived up to the hype. Fang motioned for us to take a seat on the other couch. It felt great to sit back and relax. There wasn't much in the apartment: two beat-up couches and a few milk crates sprawled out in the middle of the floor where wooden planks stretched over the top to form a makeshift coffee table. A few more wooden containers were stacked on the other wall where a small black-and-white TV sat on top, where they were watching a rerun of, I Love Lucy—which reminded me of Mom, who used to watch this show. His place wasn't extravagant: a small bathroom on one end and a kitchen that wasn't much larger than the living room but contained all the essentials—refrigerator, stove, sink, and a few cabinets to keep pots, pans, and dishes. I'm guessing the other door led to his bedroom.

All in all, his place wasn't half bad. I was a little shocked because everything was in its place. Fang was a neat freak if you asked me, and I liked that.

We relaxed and sank onto the couch. I was feeling right at home. "So, Fang, what made you decide to become a ghost hunter?" I could tell the others had no clue by the expressions on their faces.

"Great question, no one's ever asked." He smiled and looked at the others, who shrugged. Huh, I guess they all just assumed Fang wanted to keep his reasons private. "I became obsessed years ago. It was my fifteenth birthday party, two days before Halloween. My mom's friend Rebecca was helping set things up. My dad didn't want anything to do with that sort of stuff. I guess he was busy hanging out in the local tavern." He frowned.

I knew the feeling; I didn't know anything about my father, either. I only knew what my mother had told me, and I was smart enough to know I could only believe some of what she had to say. They weren't on the best of terms.

"The party was lame . . . okay, it had turned downright boring. I was glad Rebecca was there since she saved the day. She gathered us around the table and dimmed the lights. She told us about how her mother had been ill and passed when she was sixteen. It wasn't easy being raised by a man, she told us." He paused, then tilted the water glass to his lips.

"What she told us after that changed my life. Her mother came to visit every night. They would sit on the bed together and talk."

"That's impossible. You said her mother had died."

"She did. Rebecca said her mother would appear out of nowhere. She helped with homework, advice about boys, how to handle her father. You name it, they talked about it. We were glued to her every word as she mysteriously told her story. After everyone had left, I thanked her for saving my party and sharing her story. She assured me it was not just a story, that it had really happened. Rebecca and I became friends, and no, not in a romantic way." He blushed. "She was pretty hot for an older woman. No, she hung out at our house two or three times a week. She shared so many stories about her and her mom, and with each story, my interest grew. To the best of my knowledge, she still gets visits from her mother. It's because of Rebecca that I became interested in the supernatural." He paused again. "I feel like I owe it to her to prove to the world that ghosts exist, if that makes any sense."

The door burst open, and my heart skipped a beat. I was convinced I would see Rebecca, but instead, Dee strolled through, carrying an eight-pack of sixteen-ounce bottles of Pepsi.

Every time I was around Dee, my knees felt weak, and I got this weird feeling in the pit of my stomach. Gabe strolled in next, and I couldn't help but notice the super-sized large pizza box in his hands. He placed it on top of the homemade coffee table, and when he opened the lid, it covered the entire surface. The pizza must have been twenty-eight inches in diameter. It smelled fantastic, and my mouth began to water. The pizza was smothered in cheese, pepperoni, and ham. Oh, I was in heaven. Those were my favorite toppings.

Gabe flopped on the other end of the couch as Dee tossed around some paper plates and napkins. I couldn't help but notice the large stack of napkins in the kitchen, all of them printed with the Snack Shack logo. I guess Fang frequents that place. I watched as Dee pulled the drawer open and grabbed a bottle opener. I heard the hiss of air escape as she popped the tops of the Pepsi bottles. She quickly dispersed a bottle to each of us. I made sure to say thank you and moved over, allowing enough room for her to squeeze in between Gannon and me.

I couldn't wait to sink my teeth into this pizza. I opened my mouth and took a large bite. My taste buds tingled. The crust was cooked to perfection, with just the right amount of sauce, cheese, and toppings. They weren't kidding—this was the best pizza I'd ever tasted.

Dee rolled back and took a seat next to Gabe. "Thanks, babe." I watched as the two of them kissed on the lips.

My heart exploded. I thought Dee and I were a couple. *Oh, who was I kidding?* I was in disbelief. I should have known better. I thought back to last night when she helped me to my feet and steadied me as we walked back to Fang's. She winked at me, did she? She was friendly, nothing more. I guess I thought there was more because I *wanted* more. Gannon laid a hand on my shoulder and shot me a frown and mouthed, "sorry."

He could tell I was hurting. How could I have been such an idiot? *Why would a pretty girl like Dee want to be with me?* I took another large bite of my pizza. This night couldn't be over soon enough. I licked some of the sauce from my fingers, then wiped my chin. "That was good, thank you."

"Have another slice," Gabe offered.

"Thanks, but I-I ate on campus before I came here." I tried to keep calm. I didn't want anyone to know I was in pain.

"Gerald, we're going to The Blue Owl Inn this coming weekend for a ghost hunt. We would love it if you and Gannon could join us."

"Sure, that sounds—"

I cut Gannon off midstream, "I can't. Not this Saturday. Ah . . ." I stumbled to come up with a good lie, "Bates is coming into town, my friend from high school." I smiled. "I plan to show him around campus."

"He's more than welcome to join us, too. The more, the merrier," Fang said.

"Yea, we would love to meet Bates," Angel said.

"No, I promised him a day of fun." I stood and felt it was time I leave.

Gannon rose to his feet and placed a hand on my shoulder. "You okay?"

The others looked at me as if they had said something wrong. Donnie's eyes pleaded for me to join them this weekend. "Are you sure you can't make it?" Dee's voice almost begged me to change my mind.

"I'm sorry, I guess I'm not cut out for this sort of thing." I took a few steps toward the door. Gannon stretched out his arms in disbelief and to signal to the others as if he didn't know what was going on. "I'm sorry," I repeated, opened the door, and proceeded outside. Gannon followed, as did Fang.

"Gerald," Fang stopped me at the door. "If you change your mind, we're meeting here at eight p.m. I'd love it if you showed. Bring Bates, too."

"Thank you for the pizza and the invitation." I turned and proceeded down the stairs.

"I'm not sure what's going on, but I'll be in touch," Gannon blurted out. "Sorry, it was nice to meet you all."

Gannon's voice echoed over my shoulder, and he followed me down the stairs.

"Gerald. Gerald, slow down. Wait! Hold up, dude."

I paused at the bottom. "I'm a fool. I thought I was brilliant, but I'm nothing more than a foolish little boy. Why would a pretty girl like that want to be with me?" I spat out.

"Ah, man. I'm sorry. I know you thought she was your girlfriend. I feel bad. Is there anything I can do?"

"I want to go home." There wasn't much more to say. I hurt all over. *How could I have been so naïve?*

We had just cleared the alley when I felt a few drops of rain pat me on the shoulder. *Great, could this night get any worse?*

That's when the heavens opened, and the cold, torrential rain pelted us all the way back to our dorm.

CHAPTER EIGHT

I lay there tossing and turning, staring at the ceiling. I guess sleep was out of the equation. I had misunderstood the situation between Dee and me, though if I were honest with myself, it wasn't the first time I'd done something like this, either. I remembered back in tenth grade, and there had been a new girl named Janice. I thought I might have a chance with her. She was tall with beautiful legs, and she wore a lot of dresses to show them off. It was the first time I noticed a girl. She had short red hair, and freckles dotted her cheeks. Her smile drove me crazy. We'd started chatting daily, and I'd gotten excited. I felt this connection between us. I even walked her to some of her classes, and I thought we had become more than friends. When the fall sock hop was coming up, I asked her to go with me, and much to my surprise, she already had a date. I never spoke to her again.

It puzzled me. I thought Dee and I had a similar connection. I guess I was wrong again. So, last night on the rainy walk home, I decided to keep to myself and leave the ladies alone. It's easier that way. If I don't put myself out there, I won't get hurt. I even ignored Gannon for a little while, only because I was embarrassed to talk with him, and knowing he was right and I was wrong didn't help. I checked the mail slots daily, hoping Bates would return my letter, but I wasn't even sure he read mine.

The first week ended—go to class, study, eat became my daily routine. The weekend was long and tedious. Gannon respected my space and understood my situation. He even sat a row behind me in class. I checked a few books out of the library and took them back to my room to study.

I was enjoying learning in college. I found it more challenging than high school.

The second week started, and I was staying true to my word and keeping my distance from everyone. I was content with myself. The idleness and boredom of being alone was something I'd grown accustomed to—especially since I spent most of my high school days alone.

One evening I returned a few books to the library and decided to check out the third floor. I wasn't sure why. I guess I wanted to prove that I was not a ghost magnet, as Fang had stated. The room was empty, just like the night I met the alien—no ghosts here. I wandered around, going up and down every aisle. I even stopped where the books had been lying on the floor that night. Nothing, just me. I waited for five, maybe ten minutes before I had enough and went back to Deacon Hall.

My room loomed large and empty. Funny how I haven't seen or heard much from Kim, and I was getting the feeling he was avoiding me. Maybe he thought I didn't believe his ghost tale in the cafeteria. Oh well, I wasn't going to dwell on it. It gave me the space I needed.

My studies were going better than I expected. For once, I felt like I was learning at record speed, and I liked the way my professors pushed me. It wasn't easy like high school, and I found myself working for my knowledge. I crawled into bed and stared at the ceiling. *The past three weeks have been great, but I feel like part of me is still missing.*

Dawn broke, the mornings were colder now—a layer of frost lined the windows. I showered, dressed quickly, and I was off. I passed Gannon, nodded, and continued down the hallway. He called to me, but I didn't stop. I just continued and went to my quiet spot in the Eagles Nest, set my tray down, and began to eat.

The sound of shuffling feet on the other side of the table startled me from my breakfast. "Do you plan on hiding from me forever?" I recognized Dee's voice.

I grimaced. She found me. I shot her a quick nod and stuffed some eggs into my mouth. Dee set her tray down across from mine. "Please talk to me?"

I looked up briefly and raised an eyebrow. I didn't know what to say or do, and a bigger part of me wanted to run.

"I spoke with Gannon and made him tell me what was bothering you, so don't get upset with him." I looked away for a moment, then lowered my head. I was feeling a bit betrayed, but a small part of me was glad that this was out in the open.

"I like you, Gerald, as a friend, but that means I care about you. I'm sorry if you thought there was something more between us. I've been dating Gabe for two years. I like him, and he likes me. We're good for each other. I hope you understand."

I tried to clear my mind. I may have an IQ of 159, but that doesn't help me now. "I like you," I blurted out. *God, why did I say that?* I regretted the words the minute they left my lips. Her arm stretched across the table, and her hand felt soft on top of my hand. My eyes darted to hers. She looked me full in the eyes. I could tell she was sad.

"I'm sorry," I whispered, staring at my tray.

"Look at me, Gerald." Her gaze locked on. "We can be friends, and that can be special in itself." She gave me a crooked smile. "Don't you want to be friends?"

I nodded and gave her a wry smile.

"Then stop avoiding me," Dee said and sounded upset. I worked on another slice of bacon, not sure how to respond. Gannon put his tray next to mine and patted my shoulder to let me know all is forgiven.

For the first time in my life, I had friends who cared about me. I had friends. A warm feeling welled up in my chest. I had waited a lifetime for a moment like this. They forgave me for my selfish attitude. I was pouting like a child, and I knew it. I came to college to grow up, and now I needed to act like an adult. It was time to grow up.

I put my arm around Gannon and pulled him close to me. "Thank you for putting up with me."

"That's what friends do." He paused. "We're good?"

I beamed at Gannon. "Thanks. And yes, we're good." I then looked across the table to Dee. "I'm sorry for acting the way I have."

She smiled, and it was so nice to see her smile again. "Let's put it behind us. I prefer to live in the present, not the past."

“Thank you, thank you both,” I choked out, swallowing my pride.

“The others were worried about you, too. You’ll want to save an apology for them. Oh, and they won’t be as forgiving as Gannon and me.” She chuckled.

“Do you have any plans this weekend?” Gannon asked.

“Not really, what’s up?”

“We’re heading back to the Blue Owl Inn tomorrow night. Would you like to join us?” Dee asked.

“I went last time, and it was awesome.” Gannon’s eyes widened as he grinned from ear to ear.

Wow, he went without me? My instinct was to be upset—Gannon had joined the group and didn’t tell me! *What the heck.* I felt betrayed again. *Be calm*, I repeated in my head. “I’ll see how much homework I have, and if I can swing it . . .” I remained calm. “What time are you meeting?”

“We’re getting together around seven, and I really hope you’ll come.” Dee stood and smiled, then grabbed her tray. “Sorry, I have an early class. See you tomorrow?” I nodded once and watched her move toward the door.

“Don’t mess this up, man. You’re getting a second chance,” Gannon offered.

“When did you start hanging with ghost hunters?”

“When you started avoiding everyone,” he snapped. “It just happened. One night I bumped into Gabe, Sam, Donnie, and the girls while having dinner, and they invited me to join them. We talked, and one thing led to another, and the next thing I knew, we're out searching for ghosts. It was a lot of fun and a bit scary, too."

"You do know that ghosts aren't real?"

"I listened to some weird stuff that night. You might want to come and see for yourself."

"But did you see any ghosts?" I raised a brow and had apparently stumped Gannon with that question. I watched as his mouth opened and then closed, his eyes squinted, and he shrugged. I grinned, and at that moment, I knew what I had to do. I would join the group tomorrow for their ghost hunt, only because I wanted to prove that they were wasting their time. Ghosts don't exist. It wasn't because I wanted to get even with anyone. No, this experiment would be in the name of science. "I'll go, but I think the decent thing to do is to go to the library and do some research first," I said firmly.

"I would, but I have class in about thirty minutes. You go and let me know what you discovered later." Gannon shot me a sidelong look as he picked up his tray. I gave him a quick nod, and he was off.

I finished eating and snatched my tray, beginning the long walk to the return area. Once again, I was off to the library. I strolled down the sidewalk. I was not paying attention to my surroundings. I bumped into another student and quickly apologized without looking up. I cringed when I noticed the size of the guy towering over me. The sun was in my eyes, so I had to squint and saw he was a good six inches taller than me. My first instinct was to run, but instead, I smiled and wrapped my arms around Bates.

"You knucklehead," he yelled. He snagged his massive arm around my head and pulled me to his chest, making a fist as he rubbed my head. "Noogie!"

"That hurts," I cried out, and Bates laughed. The thought of my hair all tangled up and messy frustrated me. Bates tilted my head skyward. I watched as the clouds rippled past. I knew it was going to be a beautiful day, and with any luck, a little warmer.

Bates released his grip. "Don't be a baby, Gerald."

"How did you find me?" I squeaked out as he loosened his grip.

"I asked your roommate, Kim. He's an odd little fellow. He said I would find you here and gave me the directions."

"That's cool. So, what are you doing here?"

"I came to check up on my little buddy, and you sent me a letter. Besides, I had the weekend off, so I said, why not visit Gerald? Nice campus, by the way." His gaze drifted. "The girls here are hot." He smiled as a few ladies walked by. "Hello," he said, deepening his voice to impress the girls, and he raised his eyebrows a few times to flirt with them. They kept walking, and I'm glad they did.

"Where are you staying?"

"You know, for a smart guy, you can be so naïve. I'm staying with you, knucklehead. I'll take the bed, and you can have the floor. Or I'll wrestle you for the bed if you like." He bared his teeth at me. He always had an awkward smile.

My mouth went slack for a second. “Well, I guess I’ll take the floor.”

“That’s my little buddy.” He shoved my shoulder, and I leaned back to lighten the blow. That was his move. He’d done it a thousand times before. It was Bate's way of saying he liked you.

“Dang, man, it’s great to see you.” I was surprised that he took the time to drive here. I had only been a little over a month. Honestly, I should have realized Bates would do this; after all, we graduated high school together, and he was my best friend, my protector, the guy who made high school bearable. “I need to stop by the library for a second. Are you okay with that?”

“Do you ever stop reading?”

I snickered. “No, but you might be surprised to learn I’m searching for a book on ghost hunting.”

“Now that sounds cool.” Shock riddled his face. “For once, you’re talking my language.”

“I had no clue you liked paranormal stuff.”

“My grandmother used to tell me stories about ghosts. She knew one, even talked to her from time to time. Spooky, right?”

“How come you never mentioned this before?”

His face went long, and he dropped his eyes toward the ground. “It’s not something you talk about in public, unless you want people to think you’re nuts,” he whispered.

"You never worry about what people think."

"True, because I don't want to beat them up!"

"You're funny." I smacked him in the arm as we made our way to the library.

Bates shoved the library doors open and then followed me in. I glanced around, and just as I expected, there were only a few students scattered around the tables. I went straight for the stairs, stopping on the third floor. I strolled down the fourth aisle. Bates hung back while I thumbed through a few books. "They won't bite." I snickered. I wasn't exactly sure where I would find the book I needed. A shiver ran up my spine and then another one. I wasn't sure what was happening, but the day the ghost shot through me was still fresh in my mind. I quickly turned and darted out of the aisle.

Bates was relaxing at one of the tables, but he leaped to his feet when he spotted me running out of the aisle. "You okay?"

"Yeah, fine."

"You look pale. Did you see a ghost?" He laughed at his joke.

I knew he was kidding, but I wanted to be honest with him. I swallowed hard. "Yes, I think I saw one here a few weeks ago."

His jaw dropped, and his eyes widened. "Man, you're like my grandmother. Did you see a boy or a girl? Child or adult? What style of clothes were they wearing?"

"Slow down," I blurted out. "One question at a time, please." Anxiously, Bates waited for me to respond. "It was a girl; she looked about my age or a tad older. And what do you mean, what was she wearing?"

"You know, was she dressed like a cowgirl? Oh, was she dressed like a pilgrim from a hundred years ago?"

Bates always had a way of making me smile and relax. "For your information, Bates, the pilgrims came over on the Mayflower around 1620. That's 340 years ago, not a hundred."

"Oh, I see. So, you think you're smarter than me?" He lunged at me.

I sprinted down one of the aisles. I'd seen that move before, and I didn't want to be placed in another headlock. I turned and looked back at Bates, who was standing at the end of the aisle. "I can do this all day." He laughed but went back to the table to relax.

I looked around and noticed I was in the right place. Ghost hunting manuals. "How to Ghost Hunt," and "How To Tell If There's a Ghost Present." My fingers grazed the covers, stopping on "Ghost Hunting for Beginners." I inched the book from its slot, turned it over, and peered at the cover—it was nothing fancy. This was a perfect place to start. I could learn everything I needed to know before I went on my first official ghost hunt. Suddenly, the hairs on my neck rose, and I shivered. I had felt this before, though I hadn't realized it at the time. It was the same feeling as a few weeks ago. I pivoted on my heel and watched as lights began to twinkle some ten feet away. "Bates," I said, trying to stay calm.

"Bates . . ." My voice trembled much louder. "Bates . . ." I was almost ready to scream.

"What's, what's the mat— What the . . .?" he stuttered, then silence.

I looked over my shoulder, only noticing Bates' face peering around the corner. Nice, the tough guy was going to hide behind the bookcase. I turned to face the lights as they transformed into a young girl. She was close to my age, wearing a white dress that was ripped on one side. Her neck. . . Something was wrong with her neck. "Hi, I'm Gerald." I didn't know if I should smile or what. "Are you Victoria?"

Her gaze fixed on me, and she tilted her head slightly. She mouthed some words, but I didn't catch what she said.

"Can you talk?"

Her eyes fluttered, and she appeared to be in pain before she whispered, "Yes, I'm Victoria,"

I turned to look at Bates. His eyes bulged, and his mouth hung open. My anxiety rose to new heights. I was talking to a something unknown. Never in my life had I thought this would be possible. Now the science nerd in me was coming out, and all I could think about was how I could prove this. I didn't have a camera or anything to record her voice, and frustration quickly set in.

She wavered a little, blinked in and out. Oh crap. I never responded. "I'm Gerald." I tapped my fingers against my chest. She came back into focus. Her lip curled upward, and she whispered another word, "Why?"

I didn't understand. *Why what? What was she asking? Why me? Why was she here? Why was she like this?* The possibilities were endless. I took a deep breath and exhaled slowly. "What do you mean, why?"

She tilted her head to one side, gritted her teeth, and let out a loud screech, "Why?"

I covered my ears for a second. "I don't understand. What do you mean why? Please tell me." I felt helpless. I turned to face Bates, who shrugged his shoulders. I turned back to Victoria, but she was gone. The air squeezed from my lungs as I glanced left, then right. A draft of cold air rushed over me. "Victoria, come back."

Bates and I hung out for a little while longer, but it was apparent she wasn't going to return. Maybe because Bates was with me, I don't know. What disturbed me was her question, *why*? What was she asking? I had to figure this out, or it would drive me insane. Bates talked the entire way back to the dorm, and while I listened, my mind was elsewhere. *Why*? That word would haunt me.

A sudden idea occurred to me, perhaps inspired by her question. I would write a book, maybe two—one about helping spirits in some way, another book about how to cross them over, if that's even possible. I would have to follow the guidelines of science to discover the possibilities.

I pushed the door to my room open. I went straight for my desk and whipped out my notebook and started writing.

Bates frowned. "Dude, I didn't drive over here to watch you do schoolwork."

"You're right." My novel would have to wait, but I had enough time to jot down some key points before I forgot them.

Bates decided to roam the campus while I attended class. After all, I was not about to miss an opportunity to learn something. We hooked up for lunch at the Eagles Nest, where I introduced Bates to Sandy and Desmond. They didn't say much, and I guessed he was the type of boy they feared in high school. We bumped into Gannon as we left, and we decided to meet up for dinner around six.

After lunch, I showed Bates around campus. Then we met up with Gannon back at the Eagles Nest. I explained what had happened earlier at the library, though I think he doubted us a little. Instead of having to defend what I saw, I decided to change the subject. We swapped stories about our childhoods, the good and the bad. We people watched, and man, what a mix! Everyone was there, from the faculty to jocks, the hip crowd, and even single guys and gals. I used to be one of them—a loner—and I felt sorry for them, as I knew what it was like not to have friends. Couples, fraternity brothers or sorority sisters, you could always tell the difference because they wore their frat colors or logos. Bates threw out a few sarcastic comments to the ladies. I guess he thought they might like him. Sometimes he was funny, but mostly, I was embarrassed, though I'd never tell him that. While it was strange to see so many girls reject him, it did feel great to hang out with my friends.

CHAPTER NINE

The big day finally arrived. It was my first ghost hunt, and Bates was here to witness the event. Life was good. Scientifically, I wanted to prove that ghosts didn't and couldn't exist. But on the other hand, how could I explain the two events in the library? If the girl I saw wasn't an alien, she had to be a ghost. I knew of no technology that could produce a translucent figure in midair, let alone make it move and talk. Maybe one day in the future, they would be capable of generating three-dimensional images . . .

I continued to explore campus with Bates at my side for the better part of the afternoon. We wandered around the football field and athletic center because Bates enjoyed sports. I have to admit, the stadium was far more substantial than I had expected, making our high school stadium look small. I also popped into the Pryor Center, home of the literary arts department. If I was going to document my findings and publish a book, I needed to learn more about the process. I spoke with one of the professors while Bates entertained himself by showing his muscles to a pair of young college girls. I could hear them giggle at Bates' lame jokes, and I was glad he found something to keep him occupied.

Gannon stopped by my room just before dinner and threw me a black T-shirt and smiled. "Wear this."

That's when I noticed Bates and Gannon were both wearing black, something I hadn't seen until now. I thought back to high school, and come to think of it, Bates wore black shirts all the time. My mother had never approved of me wearing black unless it was for a funeral. I felt odd wearing the same color as the rest of them. I guessed this was what it was like to be a part of the team. I no longer felt like the worm. "Thanks," I said as I slipped off my shirt, replacing it with my new black one.

We grabbed our jackets and walked toward the Eagles Nest. Every direction I looked, there were pumpkins, scarecrows, and black and orange streamers. Halloween was two weeks away, and the campus had transformed into a spooky place. Mom didn't care for Halloween, so we had never put-up decorations, and I had never gone trick-or-treating.

When we entered the dining hall I noticed all the black paper crows dangling from the ceiling. Tonight, was going to be epic; I could feel it in my bones. We didn't say much over dinner; I looked up a few times and watched as we shoveled food into our mouths. I noticed Desmond and Sandy sitting alone at a small table on the other side of the cafeteria. Were they dating or were they hiding from us because we were no longer a part of their group? I didn't have time to figure that out today, but I would have to talk to them about it at some point.

I polished off my meal. *Now let this night begin*. I couldn't believe I was doing this. It was so unlike me. They said college changes people, and maybe they were right—I felt different from the day Mom dropped me off. As we walked outside, I observed the sun setting behind the mountains. The streetlights beamed across the road as we strolled down the sidewalk past fraternity row. The frat houses were dotted with Halloween decorations, and I shivered at the thought. How would I venture into an old, abandoned building if I got nervous looking at a few decorations?

I felt a cold breeze slap me in the face, and it brought me back to reality. The stars disappeared as the clouds rolled over. That could only mean one thing—a storm was brewing. We continued past the stores and the Snack Shack; the smell of the pizza hung in the air, and I was suddenly hungry again. Another block and we came to the alley, turned left, and ventured in. Lights reflecting across the street shined from the windows. For an apartment located in the middle of town, the roads were relatively quiet. I noticed a station wagon parked at the bottom of the stairs with a few boxes packed in the back. Was that Fang's car?

We walked past the empty dumpster and stopped at the bottom of the stairwell that led to the top floor. "After you," Gannon motioned. I began my ascent, past the second floor, and on my way to the top. I felt a hand rest on my shoulder, and I turned to see Bates' immense smile. I smiled back and felt more relaxed than I had all day.

I rapped my knuckles on the door three times and heard someone shuffle inside. The blind pulled back, and I caught a glimpse of Angel's smile as she opened the door.

"Hey!" She wrapped her arms around me. "Great to see you again," she whispered in my ear.

"Good to see you, too." I pulled back and motioned behind me. "This is Bates, but everyone calls him Hammer." I entered as she stepped to the side.

“Wow, Hammer’s a big boy,” Angel flirted and squeezed his biceps. Hammer was eager to flex his arm. “I never imagined you were this muscular. Do you play sports?”

“No, I’m not in college. We didn’t have the money.” Hammer sighed.

“I’m sorry, but at least you’re here today,” she replied, patting his arm as he passed.

Fang, Sam, and Donnie crouched over the table, taking inventory of their supplies. I noticed two portable reel-to-reel players and a new cassette recorder, as well as a box full of flashlights. Wow, the cassette recorders had only been out for a year or two. I knew right away Gabe’s parents must have bought it for him. I was drawn to the recorder like a magnet to metal. The boys slapped and punched me in good humor. Everyone seemed happy I showed up. I’m not sure how much they trusted me now, but I’ll earn their trust back. Gannon peeked over my shoulder to get a glimpse of the recorder. I couldn’t believe how small the cassette tapes were as I twirled one in my hand.

“Listen up.” Fang pressed the red button on the recorder. “Testing, testing, one, two, three,” he said and then pushed the stop button. He hit rewind, then play, and Fang’s voice came back through the machine. “Testing, one, two, three.”

“That’s neat.” I picked up an extra cassette tape. I guess this would mean the end of the reel-to-reel players. I just loved technology.

A firm hand pressed on my shoulder. “I’m glad you changed your mind,” Gabe said on my right.

"Thanks."

"I'm glad to see you, too," Dee said softly on my left.

I smiled. I loved having friends. I went from having one friend in high school to eight friends in a month. I had accomplished one of my goals—something I'd struggled with my entire life. A thought came to mind, and even though I was nervous, I felt I must do something, and there was no better time than now. "Can I have everyone's attention?" Everyone stopped and gazed in my direction. I swallowed hard and spoke before I had time to change my mind. "Thank you for putting up with me while I was . . ." I swallowed hard again, "kind of a jerk the past few weeks." I looked around, making eye contact with everyone in the room. The room was full of smiles, and they nodded as they accepted my apology.

"Alright, enough of the mushy stuff," Fang blurted out. "Load up the car, and let's go find some ghosts!" The room erupted in celebration, and everyone quickly grabbed the supplies. I wasn't sure what to grab, so I picked up the box of flashlights, which was heavier than I thought—it must be all the extra batteries. Hammer, of course, grabbed several folding chairs and tucked them under his arms and took off down the stairs. I followed, as did the rest of the crew. We must have sounded like a herd of cattle stampeding down the steps.

Gabe popped the back hatch of a 1960 Pontiac Catalina station wagon open. I didn't know a lot about cars, but I remembered the TV ads a few years ago. Mother had liked this car, but what would we do with a vehicle that held nine passengers? I loved the fact that it had three full bench seats. It was cool the way the second and third seats folded into the floor, too. I had assumed it was Gabe's car, and he confirmed my thought when he climbed into the driver's seat. Dee slid in beside him, and Fang called shotgun and took the front window seat. I sat the box in the back next to the chairs and climbed into the third-row seat. There was plenty of room until Hammer shoved his large butt in, forcing Gannon to the middle. At least I hung on to my window seat.

The engine roared to life, and the car lurched forward. "We're heading back to the Blue Owl Inn," Fang swirled around to announce. "You guys good with that?" A little chatter, but yes, everyone was okay with his choice. "With Gerald here, we should have better luck catching something this time."

That's when it hit me like a bag of bricks. They were counting on me to find a ghost. Or was I the bait? Suddenly, I felt used, and my insides churned with a mixture of emotions, though I immediately felt angry. They needed to know how I felt. I opened my mouth to rebel, but strange words shot out. "What's the story on this place?" I shocked myself. Why would I ask such a question? Mesmerized, I sat in silence as Fang explained.

"Glad you asked." Fang half-smiled, baring his teeth. "The Blue Owl Inn opened in 1912. It was the most prestigious hotel in the region, hosting some of the largest gatherings. Diplomats came from all over the state. Some were esteemed professors and politicians—all important people from that period. The place was owned and operated by George and Beatrice Hampton, who lived on the top floor, along with their daughter, Lily. The years passed, and rumor has it she was one hot gal. Then, in October 1929, the stock market crashed, and the Great Depression began. Over twenty-five percent of Americans were out of work. Herbert Hoover was president at the time, but he would soon be replaced by Franklin D. Roosevelt in 1932. Sorry, I'm getting off track. I'm a bit of a history buff, in case you couldn't tell." Fang chuckled.

"Don't let Fang fool you, Gerald. He's majoring in history and could definitely teach high school or college once he graduates," Sam added.

"Imagine that, Fang teaching history." Donnie laughed. I briefly smiled, then changed my expression. Education was not a funny subject, but I was impressed Fang had his major.

"Congratulations," I added.

"Thank you, now may I?" We cleared the edge of town as Fang continued, "Okay, then, in 1930, the inn fell on hard times. Money grew tight and people stopped traveling. The Hamptons needed to increase business, so they lowered prices and let students and parents stay at the hotel. Everything was fine at first, but then, on December thirteenth, a group of young men were in town for a sporting event. One of them was named Gerald." My mouth dropped, as did Gannon's. "Sorry, just kidding." Fang and the others enjoyed a good laugh. "His name was Reginald Ream, but his friends called him Reggie. Yes, the same name as Professor Ream, who teaches on campus."

"I-I'm in his class," I stuttered.

"They say that's why he's so mean. New students soon find out who he is, and they snicker behind his back when they realize he's a distant relative of the man who caused Lily's death."

"Then why do they let him teach here?" I asked.

"He didn't kill anyone, so why wouldn't they let him teach? Anyway, I'm off track again." Fang sighed. "On December thirteenth, Reggie noticed Lily in the dining hall and began to flirt with her. Later that evening, when all the guests had returned to their rooms, George was locking things up when he heard a noise coming from the kitchen. They say what he saw was horrifying. He caught his daughter Lily kissing Reggie. Her father became livid, turned, slammed the door behind him, and ran upstairs to retrieve his shotgun. Reggie and Lily followed, trying to plead their case and make him understand. Lily said she loved Reggie, but George would not stand for this. His daughter was only sixteen, almost seventeen from what I understand, but still, what did she know about love? George loaded his gun, pointed it at Reggie, and demanded he leave the hotel immediately, but Reggie refused. Beatrice tried to calm George down, but he was beyond reproach."

"He continued to point the weapon directly at Reggie, cocked the gun, and issued a final warning. The boy refused to leave, and people say that George had pulled the trigger by accident. But just as he pulled the trigger, Lily stepped in front of Reggie to protect him."

Hammer, Gannon, and I sat speechlessly. I guessed the others had heard the story before because they didn't react. "How come I didn't know this?" I asked.

"It's not something they print in the college brochure," Fang explained.

"So, he shot and killed his daughter?" I asked.

“Yes.”

“I can’t even imagine how he must have felt after shooting her.” I would have been mortified.

“They say that’s why she never crossed over. She was taken before her time, accidentally killed by her father. Several months later, George took his own life, so the case never went to trial. Legend has it, they still walk the halls of the inn, and that’s why we’re here,” Fang concluded as the car came to a stop in a gravel parking lot.

My eyes widened as I realized we’d arrived, and I peered out the window. A four-story structure with rotting wood and shoddy windows loomed over us in the dark.

CHAPTER TEN

I lifted the handle until I heard the clicking sound and slowly pushed the door open. I placed a foot on the crushed gravel. The parking lot was overgrown with weeds and brush. I stepped away from the car as the others pushed out. The nine of us gazed at the abandoned inn. I shivered in the cold evening air. Clouds raced passed as the full moon glowed ominously in the night sky, casting the illusion that the moon was resting atop one of the chimneys that graced the roofline. Something swayed in the upper window, and my eyes bulged at the moving curtain. *Was someone here? Were they watching us?* Panic raced through me. That's when I noticed the corner of the window was broken, which eased my mind. *Not a ghost, just the wind. Calm down, Gerald!*

The inn was more significant than I had expected, with four stories cascading upward with six windows on each floor stretching east to west. The craftsman design was unique for that period. The massive arches over the windows reminded me of a frown. *Was the inn sad?* I studied the building a bit before I blurted out, "If my math is correct, there are about seventy-two rooms."

"I can see why you would think that, but there are only sixty guest rooms. The top floor contained larger rooms for elite guests and the family, though we would call them suites today." He half-smiled. "On the first floor, we'll find the front desk, lobby, dining hall, kitchen, maintenance, and storage areas." He pointed in the direction of the inn. "We'll set up our command downstairs and break into four teams so we can cover all the floors. The basement's collapsed, I think, from a flood years ago. So, we can't go down there. Gerald, Hammer, this is your first ghost hunt, so try not to disturb anything. We sit, wait, observe, and record what we see and hear. Do you understand?" Hammer and I nodded. "So, what are we waiting for? Let's move," Fang barked.

Gabe, Sam, and Donnie made a beeline to the rear of the car. Hammer, Gannon, and I gathered behind the others. The back hatch was lowered, and Donnie began passing out supplies. The folding chairs were handed to Hammer, and Gannon grabbed a few smaller camping stools. I was given the box of flashlights again. Fang held one portable reel-to-reel player, and Donnie grabbed the other. Gabe carried the final package that contained the new cassette recorder, which was smaller and lighter. I couldn't wait to hear what sounds we were going to record. I felt giddy like a kid at Christmas.

The front door was chained and locked, so we walked past, heading to the side entrance where a large red sign was nailed to the door. I stopped in my tracks as I said, "Ah, the sign says no trespassing."

"It's fine, Gerald," Donnie said.

My eyes widened and I pointed back to the sign. "That's not what the sign says."

"Technically, Gerald, the sign doesn't say anything because signs can't talk. It shows us something that we have to read," Gabe said with a hint of sarcasm in his voice.

Gabe had a valid point. Signs couldn't talk. But the fact remained that we were still breaking the law by entering the building without permission. "Well, the sign shows us we can't enter without someone giving permission," I fired back and shot him my death stare.

"Gerald, we were granted admission by my father, who is the mayor." He smirked. "Now, if you all don't mind, can we get started?"

Well, that was something I didn't know. Maybe that's why Gabe had money. His father was the mayor and a politician, and things were starting to add up.

With the tap of his foot, Donnie edged the wooden door open. The moonlight cast through the dust-covered windows, shedding enough light for us to see and set up our command center. I gazed at the chestnut wainscoting that flowed halfway up the wall, which was badly faded. I moved my flashlight up and noticed the peeling paint in sections of the top half. I peered at the large wooden archway over the lobby counter. My neck stretched upward, and my mouth fell open as I stared at the beamed and coffered ceilings. *How elegant.* I wish I could have seen this inn in its glory days.

Gabe and Dee made up team one, or the joker squad as Gabe called it. They would run the operation and survey on the first floor. Sam grabbed two folding chairs, and Angel picked up a flashlight and walkie-talkie. That's when I noticed the instant Polaroid camera hanging around her neck. I had read about them, but I'd never seen one in person. You take a picture, and the black and white film rolls out and develops before your eyes. About three years ago, Polaroid came out with a color version, but this was the older model from this camera's looks. I watched as Angel and Sam headed up the stairs for the second floor—they were the sniper squad. Donnie and Gannon—the demon squad—snatched up two folding chairs and the rest of their supplies and proceeded to the third floor.

Fang, Hammer, and I would camp out on the top floor. Hammer grabbed the small camping stools while I snatched a flashlight and walkie-talkie. I had always wanted to play with one of these when I was younger, but Hammer said they were lame and for sissies. That's why I never asked my mom for a set at Christmas. Fang grabbed the reel-to-reel player, and we began our ascent to the top floor where Lily's life was supposedly taken.

Nervously, I followed Fang and Hammer to the grand staircase. The woodwork and detail of the railing were exquisite. I'd never been fascinated with architectural work until now. Maybe it was something I should study. We neared the second floor, and I couldn't help but notice the circle of salt that surrounded Sam and Angel as they sat facing each other in the middle of the hallway, and they shot us a nod. We rounded the corner and pushed our way to the third floor.

"What's the salt for?"

"They say it wards off spirits," Fang said as he continued to climb.

"But I thought we were here to find ghosts?"

"We are. Ghosts can't cross the salt line, so you're safe inside the salt circle."

"How does it work?"

"They say it creates a barrier; one a spirit isn't powerful enough to disturb."

"Do we have salt?"

"We don't need it. It's never been proven to work." Fang motioned us forward.

I cringed as a shiver rocked my body.

What an illusion. The building looked enormous from the outside, but inside, the corridors were relatively narrow and the rooms looked tiny. Darkness fell inside the stairwell. I reached into the box and flicked on the flashlight. It was easier to see, but that didn't calm my nerves. I was still on edge as we climbed up the next flight of stairs. I spotted a flicker of light coming from around the corner. My mind raced back to my experience in the library. I was about to face another ghost . . . Lily! Considering the circumstances, anything was possible. My adrenaline galloped with excitement. I took another step and paused, then slowly, I gawked around the corner. The light was coming from Donnie and Gannon's flashlight—that's what set my nerves on fire—and I half-smiled and gave a quick nod to the boys as we maneuvered past.

The last flight of stairs separated us from Lily. Now was the moment of truth. I placed my right foot on the first plank and moved my left foot up to the next board. There was a stillness in the air. Fang was two steps ahead of me when he suddenly stopped and his shoulders twitched. "Everything okay?" I asked, and I heard my voice waver.

"Something's not right . . . I can feel it. I-I can't explain it . . . it's different," he whispered back.

"What are we waiting for?" Hammer asked.

I raised a finger to my lips. "Shh."

"Turn the light off," Fang instructed.

"What? Are you kidding?" I muttered but followed orders and flicked the switch off. The stairwell collapsed into total darkness and after a few moments, our eyes adjusted to the lack of light. We stood and listened before Fang moved up a step, then paused again. It was a slow process until we crested the top landing. The room opened up to what looked like a small lobby. To the left were the family quarters—I could tell because I only noticed two doors on that side of the hallway—and several doors leading to the elite suites lined the right side.

"I don't understand . . ." Fang mumbled.

He appeared to be nervous about something, which wasn't helping me find comfort. No, quite the opposite. I turned to Hammer, who wore a broad smile and didn't seem to have a care in the world. For the first time, the thought occurred to me that we might be in danger. "What do you mean?" I asked.

"We left the doors open last time we were here, and now they're closed." Fang pointed to the family quarters.

"The wind must have closed them."

"Impossible, I used chairs to prop them open so I could listen inside the rooms." Fang pointed toward a toppled chair at the other end of the hallway. I detected a bit of panic in his voice. His footsteps echoed on the hardwood floor. We pushed our way to the middle of the landing, giving us a great view of the corridor. "Put the stools over here." He pointed to

Hammer. He turned the knob and shoved the first door open, grabbed the chair on the inside, and wedged it under the handle.

I sank my butt in the stool and was flanked by Fang and Hammer. For some reason, I felt protected being in the middle. The reel-to-reel was placed a few feet away in the center of the floor, then Fang pushed the record button, and I watched the two small reels start to spin. I ran my eyes up and down the dusty, cobweb-filled hallway. There were no signs of life or any ghosts. Five, ten, fifteen minutes passed as we sat silently in the dark.

A cracking sound erupted from the walkie-talkie, and my head snapped to attention as I let out a squeak of surprise. "Sniper team, report."

"Are you a mouse?" Hammer nudged me in the side and smiled down at me.

"All clear."

"Demon team, report."

"Nothing here." I recognized Gannon's voice.

"Fang, report."

"The air's electric, too much tension. Everyone stay alert. Lily knows we're here and she's not happy." Fang relayed.

I felt a slight pressure on my shoulder, and I jumped, only to find Hammer's hand poised above my shoulder, sporting a grin on his face. "God, don't do that!"

He snickered again.

An hour passed, and we checked in every twenty minutes with command. I started to feel silly for sitting in the dark in an abandoned building, waiting for Lord knows what to appear. I wondered if we should open all the doors, but I relied on Fang for guidance. The night was slipping away—I could be at my dorm right now, studying or writing in my journal. My left arm twitched, followed by a weird tingling sensation—the kind you get when a part of your body falls asleep. The feeling rolled upward toward my neck. Something didn't feel right. I glanced, jumped to my feet, and screamed as I whooshed the spider off my shoulder. "Oh God! Oh God, that was gross!" I shivered.

"You'll survive," Hammer said as I watched him squash the spider under his foot.

"Don't move," Fang whispered and pointed to the other end of the hallway.

I tilted my head sideways, and the air oozed out of my lungs as a gust of wind passed through me, dropping me to one knee. I'd forgotten all about the spider. Delirious, I tried to stand, and I felt Hammer's hand try to brace me.

"We need back-up and a camera on four," Fang whispered into the walkie-talkie.

"Ten-four," Gannon replied.

I hoisted myself up with the help of Hammer. My eyes watered, and I blinked a few times to clear them and gazed down the corridor to see a floating candle hover in midair. Who was holding the candle? Was this Lily?

The flame and candle vanished, and a small, blurry, opaque mass appeared in its place. I gasped and swallowed hard. *She's here.* I could see my breath in the night air as the temperature plunged. The world froze, time stopped, but then righted itself in seconds. My knees wobbled. The object closed the distance between us and tripled in size. I heard whispers behind me, both male and female. I think everyone was here to witness this encounter, yet I felt alone.

The mass transformed, taking the shape of a girl who I assumed was Lily. "Hello," I choked out.

She slightly tilted her head to check me out. She was beautiful and stood about five feet tall. She wore a soft pink dress that flowed to the floor, brushing the tops of her bare feet. I looked upward and noticed the large red stain in her mid-section, her light cream-colored skin contrasting against the deep red. *I didn't know ghosts could display color.* She frowned, knowing I could see her wounds. At the moment, I felt like the worm again, and I was about to be devoured. I needed to muster up my courage. I tried to remain stoic and sharp. Here was the chance to prove to myself that I could do anything. I wasn't the little boy that my mother knew. Like a sailor on a wet deck, I found my footing. "Are you Lily?" I asked firmly.

I expected a response, though I'm not sure why. "Sound gentler," Fang whispered in a calm voice.

I jumped, startled by Fang's voice—I'd forgotten I wasn't alone. "Lily," I half-smiled, "I'd love to get to know you." I bit my lip and swayed back and forth.

Our eyes locked, and I noticed sadness and pain in her eyes and a face full of shame. She had missed so much in her life, cut short all because of a boy. Something tugged at my brain, and then I felt her presence inside me as she forced her way inside my mind. *How was this possible?* I pushed my index finger to my forehead where a shooting pain seared from within. I winced, took a step back, but she closed in, inches from my face. "*Why are you here?*" She gave me an innocent smile as her voice echoed in my head.

I was astounded. Our thoughts were intertwined. Lily stilled me with her smile. I furrowed my brow. Her question burned deep. I pretended to understand and thought to myself, *I'm here to help you.* I needed to know if she could read my thoughts.

She frowned. "*You can't help me.*"

"*Yea,*" my mouth flew open, but no words escaped. We were communicating telepathically where she could read my thoughts and I could read hers. Wow, this was beyond anything I could have ever imagined. "*I would like to try.*" I smiled softly.

"*No one can help me. Leave this place now.*"

"*Tell me what you need, and I promise to help.*"

"I'm tired. I'm stuck in this house. I want to move on. I want this to end. Can you help me?" The room started to warm.

"*I don't know how.*" I frowned. *"But I'll go to the library, do some research, and learn. Yes, I will try to help you move to the other side."* I nodded.

"Gerald, talk to her," Fang whispered in my ear.

Slowly, I turned in a subtle way. I raised my hand to let him know to back off and mouthed the words, "everything's okay."

I could tell he and the rest of the crew were frustrated with the silence and growing impatient. I turned to Lily. "*Can we talk out loud so all the others can hear?*" I begged.

"*They've been here before. They're not nice.*"

"I understand," I said out loud. "Lily's reading my thoughts, and I hers." I wanted to make sure everyone knew I was communicating with Lily. A brilliant flash of light filled the room, followed by the sound of a zipper. Angel had taken a picture. The film made a funny sound as a photo slid out of the case. "Stop." My words sounded harsher than expected.

I turned to face Lily, and I saw her tremble with her back to me. "I'm sorry; it's only a picture." I paused and inhaled through the tension. "Breathe," I whispered as I took a long breath. "Thanks for not leaving. Can you explain how my friends were mean to you?" The others scuttled around, shocked by the accusation.

"This is my home." Her voice was soft, yet sounded heavy with sadness as it floated through the room. The others remained silent and listened intently. "They moved my furniture and disrespected my space. They made strange noises and called out to me. They shined flashlights here and there and disturbed me when I was sleeping. They've even left garbage behind." A tear traced down her cheek.

"We're sorry," Fang pleaded for forgiveness. "I never thought about it like that." He frowned. "Please forgive us?"

After a long moment of silence, Lily said. "I forgive you as God would forgive you."

"Thank you. I promise we'll try harder."

"Gerald," Lily said, her voice calm and sweet. I was taken aback that she remembered my name. I didn't know if I should be honored or frightened.

"Yes."

"You said you would help."

"I will tr—"

"Gerald, don't make promises we can't keep, not with the dead," Fang interrupted.

"I'm not dead," she hissed. "How dare you say that to me?"

"I'm sorry, truly sorry." Fang bowed his head as if to beg for forgiveness.

"He meant no harm. He's foolish. Forgive him." I waited but received no response. "I promise I'll go to the library. There has to be something on the subject of crossing a spirit over."

"No, no, that's forbidden," Fang retorted. "We don't interfere."

"You're trying to trick me." The rage in Lily's eyes frightened me as the temperature plunged and the wind howled. "Get out of my house; get out now!" she screamed. The others started to back away, and I heard footsteps on the stairs. Glancing over my shoulder, I noticed Hammer was still here, wearing a larger-than-life smile. Donnie and Gannon had positioned themselves for a fast exit in case one was needed. I was glad to see Fang had not abandoned me, but the girls had vanished, most likely gathering their things and heading for the car.

"I didn't trick you . . . I didn't know there were rules. Please forgive me," I admitted and took a step back toward the stairs. I felt terrible. I truly wanted to help. I picked up the stool and flashlight and placed another foot in the direction of the steps. Hammer grabbed the other seat, and Fang pressed the off button on the reel-to-reel, snatched the unit up, and pushed his way toward the stairs.

"Leave before I tell my daddy." Her tone frightened me. "He doesn't like boys calling on me. I'm going to tell him you like me." Her laugh turned evil, and a chilling sensation rushed over me. I knew I had upset her. It was unintentional, but nevertheless, the damage was done.

I wasn't sure what kind of power ghosts had, but I knew I didn't want to meet her father. He had already killed his daughter. Hammer pulled me back and told me to run. I sprinted down the three flights of stairs, never once looking back. Fang nipped at my heels, barking at me to go faster. I leaped off the bottom step and across the main lobby floor and darted out the door.

The crisp night air punched me in the face. I stopped running when I reached the car; Gabe, Dee, and Angel, and the rest of the crew were already inside. I tossed the chair into the back and watched Fang do the same with the recorder.

I looked back to the open door. "Where's Hammer?"

My eyes darted upward. An explosion of light filled the fourth-floor window and beamed out over the parking lot. I heard screaming within. Soon, Hammer barreled out of the side door, slamming it behind him.

He stopped short of the car, bent over to rest his hands on his knees, and started to laugh. “Wow, what a rush.”

CHAPTER ELEVEN

A blanket of fog diminished our view of the hotel. I burst from the car and ran to Hammer. "Are you alright?" I watched as he regained his breath and righted himself.

"That was fantastic," he screeched. His eyes were wide like a crazed man. I'd never seen him like this. He was having the time of his life while the rest of us ran for ours. "What's next?"

"We go home, review the tapes, and decide what to do with the evidence," Fang explained. "The photo . . . Where's the picture?" He scrambled toward Angel, who frowned.

She stretched out her hand to offer him the print. He exploded with excitement as he snatched the film from her hand. The stunned reaction was all I needed to see to know that something was wrong with the picture. "What happened? I-I don't understand." His frustration quickly turned to anger. "How could this happen?" he fumed as he handed me the photo of the blurry hallway.

"It looks like someone ran their hand over the film, creating a glob of chaos." The words came out harsher than I expected.

"Thanks, Gerald, for your commentary on the obvious."

I hung my head, feeling horrible for my sharp tongue. "Sorry."

"Forget it, let's head to the house."

"What do you mean we go home?" Hammer asked. "We have to stay or find another place that's haunted. That was awesome."

We all enjoyed a good laugh. "Sorry, bud, but I've had enough of the paranormal for one evening." I patted Hammer on the shoulder as I climbed back into the car. I did have one concern, and I needed to get that off my chest. "So why didn't Lily follow us?"

Fang shot me a sidelong glare. "Entities, ghosts, orbs, whatever you want to call them are bound to a certain area. Once you leave their boundary, you're safe. In this case, Lily's confined to that hotel." He pointed over his shoulder to the upper floor and placed the reel-to-reel at his feet. "As I mentioned upstairs, you don't interfere with the supernatural. We can't help her. It's an unwritten rule of ghost hunters."

"Are you saying it's not possible?"

"Yes. I mean, no . . . it's possible to help them, I guess. But I don't do that, we don't do that. I look for ghosts so I can prove they exist."

"Do you mind if I try to help? I mean, maybe we could do both. Hunt them and help them?"

"I don't know, Gerald. I don't know much about the process. We'll talk about it later, okay?"

"Sounds great."

Why ghost hunt if you can't help them?

The dense fog gave the hotel a spooky appearance. I glanced at the top floor and noticed a small orb glowing in the left window. I knew that had to be Lily, so I smiled and waved as we pulled away.

I couldn't wait to go to the library. I had research to conduct. The ride back to Fang's was filled with excitement and chatter about how this was the first time they had seen a real ghost. I think disbelief was a better way to describe how they must have felt. I know that's how I felt the first time I met Victoria.

My mind wandered, mesmerized by the fact that I might be able to help Lily and Victoria. I came to college to get an education and make friends, and here I was trying to figure out how to help spirits cross to the other side. There was something about this subject that intrigued me, maybe because they were damsels in distress. No, perhaps because neither of them had asked to die.

A month ago, I didn't believe in ghosts. Now I'd met two. Wow, it sure was strange how things turned out. I mean, how many spirits were out there? Could I help them all? I needed to write a novel to describe the process. That was the first thing I was going to do when I got home.

The car jerked to a halt and soon, everyone chipped in by grabbing boxes and chairs. I followed the others up the stairs and set the box in the kitchen. Fang placed the reel-to-reel on the coffee table, and Gabe set the cassette recorder beside it. The boys re-wound the tapes as the rest of us watched the spinning wheel with great anticipation. My excitement level increased as the seconds ticked away. Click, and the button popped up, letting us know the cassette was ready, though the reel-to-reel was much slower. Fang pushed play, and we heard little to no noise. Fang pushed fast-forward and the tape squealed. Seconds later, he hit stop, then play, and voices blared from the speaker. It took me back to the inn. I could see everything unfold in my mind.

Moments passed before my voice echoed through the machine. I listened intently. *Oh, my goodness, do I really sound like that?* Yet, I still needed to listen to the conversation. My eyes popped when I heard Lily's voice echo through the speaker and the room erupted in cheers. We had recorded her voice—it was plain, clear, and precise, and it was Lily. But how do we prove that to the world?

I hated to ruin the moment, but I had to point out the obvious being a guy of science. "We need a home movie camera." All eyes turned to me and I frowned. "This voice recording means nothing without evidence that this was not one of us talking."

"What are you saying? You were there; you saw her; you spoke to her. This tape's the real deal." Fang sounded annoyed, and I understood why.

"I can relate to what you're saying, but how do we convince the world that this is the voice of a ghost named Lily? We need more; we need to record a movie with sound. Showing all of us, so we have indisputable evidence that none of us are talking or moving objects." I glared at each of them.

"Ah, maybe we could see if Lily could hold something for us? Record a floating candle?" Gannon murmured.

"Great idea, but I'm sure she won't find that amusing." I grinned.

"I'll buy the camera and projector tomorrow, maybe another cassette player or two. I'll tell my folks it's for a school project, so I'm sure they won't object," Gabe offered.

Hammer smiled. "So, we're going back?"

"It looks that way . . ." Fang hinted. "It's frustrating because we all saw Lily, right?" My head bobbed in harmony with the others. "And now you're telling me that the evidence we collected is no good."

"I'm sorry, but think about how the scientific community will look at us when we only play her voice." I raised an eyebrow.

"I see your point. I only hope Lily appears tomorrow," Fang said with a sidelong glare.

"Awesome, we're going back. I can drive home Monday morning." Hammer beamed and bounced on the balls of his feet.

Gabe smiled. "I'm fine with that." I watched as Dee pulled him close. It still stung a little watching the two of them, but I get it. Maybe one day I'd have a girlfriend. I found myself staring at Angel and wondered what it would be like to kiss a girl as pretty as her. Pain seared my left arm as Gannon landed a jab.

"Hey, that hurt."

"You okay?"

"Yeah, fine. Sorry, just thinking."

"Yeah, I see who you were thinking about." He chuckled. "Best of luck with Angel."

I shot Gannon a quirky grin.

Things wrapped up quickly, and the others agreed to go back tomorrow evening. I hoped Gabe could land the video recorder; then maybe, with a little luck, we could film Lily. I was excited about the possibilities, yet another part of me was sad because we were about to invade Lily's privacy again.

"I guess I need to head to the library." I motioned Hammer and Gannon toward the door and said my goodbyes. I hoped to find a book that would shed some light on crossing a spirit over to the other side. The cold night air slapped my face as the door closed behind me. Hammer leaped down the stairs, his feet hitting every other step. I took my time. The last thing I needed was to fall and break my neck. We made a beeline across town and straight to the library. I remember reading in the freshman manual that the library stayed open until two a.m. on Friday and Saturday and closed at midnight on other days. Luckily for us, it was a Saturday night. I imagined the place would be empty, except for a few nerds like myself.

We rounded the last street corner and briskly walked to the large glass doors. Hammer pushed the door open with ease. My thin jacket wasn't cutting it and I couldn't wait to get inside where it was warm. My body trembled as I slammed into the wall of heat. It wouldn't take long to warm up. I smiled and started toward the stairs with Gannon on my heels.

"Hey, I think I'm going to hang here, unless you need me," Hammer pleaded and nudged his head toward a couple of girls sitting alone at one of the tables.

I nodded and started my climb to the third floor. Like always, the floor was vacant. Gannon and I stopped, glancing at the signs at the end of the bookcases. I'm not sure why I hesitated; maybe it was the eerie feeling that warned me that something wasn't right. I couldn't see anyone, but I had this feeling that someone was here. We took a few steps and peered down the first aisle, then the second, making our way across the entire floor. I walked down the last row at the back of the library, only to confirm we were alone.

"Shh." I raised a finger to my lips. "Did you hear that?" Gannon looked around and shook his head. Quietly, I placed one foot in front of the other and slowly started moving back to the third floor's common area. I heard something drag on the floor. I stopped and motioned for Gannon to stop. I grew nervous; we looked front and back, up and down. The scraping sound continued and ended with a soft thud. We heard it several times before it finally ceased. We took a few more steps to the end of the aisle. My heart was pounding so loud I thought it was going to leap from my chest.

I was ready to peek around the corner. Just as I moved, Gannon grabbed my arm and pulled me back. "Oh crap," I whimpered. My head spun around, and I locked gazes with his wide eyes.

"Let's go home."

"We can't leave now. Victoria's here." I tried to be brave for Gannon's sake, but inside, I was petrified. I thought of how fast Lily's attitude had changed—how she went from soft-spoken to evil laughter. *What if Victoria flipped on me? One wrong move and we could get hurt, or worst, killed.* I was beginning to respect their supernatural powers.

Gannon shook his head. I guess he'd had enough. Who could blame him for feeling like that? I turned around, curled my fingers around the edge of the hardwood shelf, and forced myself to gaze around the corner. "What the heck?" I whispered as I slowly pushed myself out into the open space. I could feel Gannon gasp behind me.

The chairs were placed upside down on top of the tables, not just one table but two, sixteen chairs in all, as if the library were about to close and the chairs needed to be put up. I supposed that's possible. You'd think they would have made an announcement. Maybe I missed it. But who could have done this, and why? I hadn't seen anyone. Was this a warning? What did it mean?

I walked to the front landing, stood at the top of the staircase, and gazed back over the floor. If there was someone here other than Gannon and me, we were going to find them. Gannon nervously made his way to the rear of the room. We looked up and down each aisle, working our way to the middle, trying to find someone, something to make sense of what we were seeing.

Then I heard someone trying to cover her laugh. With any luck, the laughter would belong to Victoria. I raised a finger to my lips for Gannon to see and pointed in the direction of aisle seven—lucky number seven as they say. Gannon went down eight, trying to flank whoever it was. I waited with anticipation, making sure no one could get past me or off this floor without us seeing. Of course, if this were a ghost, they could just disappear, and we would never know.

A clatter arose. I heard books crashing to the floor, then a scream. "Got ya," Gannon yelled, and the scuffle was over. It was a female, her voice familiar, yet I couldn't put a face to her voice. Gannon removed her from the aisle. I was stunned. I hadn't seen her in weeks. What was she doing on the third floor?

"Sandy," I hollered. "What the heck are you doing here?" I paused. "We were in the middle of trying to catch a ghost."

"You fool." Sandy laughed. "It was me; I stacked the chairs. Don't be so gullible." She beamed with pride. "This place isn't haunted like those boys would have you believe. They're playing you and Gannon for fools and setting you up to embarrass you in front of everyone."

Stunned by her accusations, I shook my head. "No, no, no, I don't believe you." Could this be some elaborate joke to make the brainiac kid look like an idiot? "I'm not buying it," I snapped.

She shrugged with a smirk. "It's your life."

Could this be high school all over again? I thought they were my friends. Now I found myself having doubts. *After all this time, could I still be the worm?*

"Don't listen to her," Gannon urged. "She doesn't know what she's saying."

I didn't know who to believe at this point. The scuffle of shoes approached behind me. I spun quickly to see Hammer walking up with a lovely girl hanging on his arm.

A smile cracked my face—it didn't take Hammer long to meet someone. I wish I could talk to girls like he could. He may not be the brightest person I know, but Hammer had many qualities that I wish I had, like convincing a girl to kiss him.

"What's going on?" Hammer asked, concern riddled his voice.

"Someone's playing games." I pointed to Sandy. I grimaced, feeling like a child who'd just tattle-taled to the teacher. Hammer's face darkened, the muscles tightened in his neck, and his eyes narrowed. I'd seen this look before.

"I didn't mean anything by it." Sandy cowered. "I thought it would be funny," she continued and inched her way toward the stairs as a tear trickled down her face. "I'm sorry . . ." She dashed for the stairs.

"You're mean," the girl hanging on Hammer's arm hissed, then bolted after Sandy, probably going to comfort her.

"Great," Hammer shouted in frustration. "She was nice."

"Sorry, man," Gannon blurted out and gawked at me.

"What?" I asked, trying to play innocent. "I didn't do anything." My heart gave me a little kick. "Okay, I might have overreacted a little." I pinched my fingers together as an example. "But why would she say those things?"

"I don't know, maybe because we are hanging out with the cool kids and she's not?" Gannon threw his hands up.

"Did you find your books?" Hammer asked. He always had a way of moving on, letting go, and not holding a grudge, unlike me. I tended never to forget; I stored my thoughts in a memory bank deep inside.

I went back to the aisle and started looking for books that might help me help the spirit world—finding several that may guide me in the right direction. I latched on to two books and started for the stairs.

"Ready." I proceeded to the checkout.

The walk back to the dorm was quiet, which I blamed on the cold weather. Fatigue set in, and I couldn't wait to curl up in my warm blankets.

CHAPTER TWELVE

Snoring woke me from a deep sleep. I noticed Hammer curled up on the floor with a blanket wrapped around his mid-section and bare feet dangling from under the covers. *How could he be warm?* I sat up, sending a book crashing to the floor as it rolled off my chest. I must have fallen asleep while I was reading.

"Shh." Kim sounded frustrated, his comforter rustled, and he turned his back to me. I'd forgotten all about my roommate. We hadn't talked in weeks, and part of me wondered what he'd been up to. Had I been a bad roommate? I wasn't sure it mattered; he seemed to have found his footing with college life without me.

I pushed my way out of bed, stepped over Hammer, and made my way down the hall to the bathroom. A level of excitement flowed within. We're going back to the Blue Owl Inn, and I couldn't wait to talk with Lily. I had questions only she could answer.

I finished my business, strolled down the hallway, stopping once to knock on Gannon's door. There was no answer. Maybe he got an early start to the day or was still snoozing. I moseyed back to my room and removed the book from the floor. I turned it over and opened the pages and began to read and take notes. I was determined to write the best ghost hunting spirit guide of all time. Nothing would stop me. I'd met two ghosts and talked to them, so who better to help me write this story than myself?

Why me? The thought never occurred to me until now. *Why or how do I attract ghosts?* I'd have to ask Fang and see if he had any thoughts on the subject.

I worked on my novel until the early afternoon when I forced Hammer to wake up—which wasn't an easy task. Gannon popped in saying he was heading to the Eagles Nest, and I told him that as soon as Hammer was ready, we'd meet him over there. After freshening up, we finally made our way to the dining hall. Much to my surprise, we found Gannon sitting with Sandy. After a few awkward moments, she broke the silence. "I'm sorry about last night," she whispered, her voice sincere.

"For what you did? Or for what you said?" I wasn't as forgiving as Gannon. What she said was hurtful.

"For both." She frowned. "I was only trying to be funny, but I want you guys to be careful around that group."

"We will," Gannon interrupted before I had a chance to respond.

I nodded, then accepted her apology. I didn't say I was sorry for overreacting because I didn't think I owed her one. She should be lucky I received hers, though I will store the experience away in the back of my mind. We finished our meal and made our way back to the dorm.

Winter had come early as the frigid air engulfed us. I wondered if this would hamper our plans for the evening. It also brought several more questions to mind. *Do ghosts feel the cold and heat like humans?*

I watched Gannon and Hammer play cards. You would think I'd be good at cards or board games, being a smart guy, but I wasn't, and from the look of things, neither was Gannon. I continued to read and take notes, my foot tapping on the floor. It's something I do when I sit for too long. I made progress on my story as the words flowed from my mind to the paper with ease.

Finally, Hammer announced it was time to go. I wasn't looking forward to the long walk to Fang's apartment, but thank goodness the wind settled down, making our walk across town cold but not gut-wrenching. We turned down the alley, and I spotted Gabe's brown station wagon parked at the base of the stairs. The others must have gathered in the apartment. Our pace heightened, and we scampered up the stairs with ease. Hammer quickly knocked on the door. I guess our big muscle man didn't like the cold weather, either.

I noticed the broad smile draped on Angel's face as the door swung open. She's always happy, and in a way, I wanted to be like her, always positive. After all, who needs negativity in their life? Gannon and I pushed forward. I looked around as the door slammed behind us. Gabe bounced to his feet, eager to show off his new video camera. It was much more significant than I expected. I couldn't wait to see the images we would capture. Excited, Gabe explained, "I told my parents we saw a ghost last night, even talked to her. My dad was skeptical, but my mother hung on my every word and believed me. I told her what you said about the need for video proof, and that was it, we were off to Radio Shack." He held up the video recorder with pride. "I got this new baby." He pushed the camera toward me. Wow, the thing was massive. "Did I mention they allowed me to buy another cassette recorder?" He handed the cassette to Gannon as I passed the camera to Hammer. Even though I was intrigued and fascinated with the machine, I didn't want to risk breaking it.

"Great, everyone's here. We can get an early start," Fang said. With the wave of his hand, he held our attention. "Same plan as last night. Gabe, Dee, you guys set up in the lobby. Sam, Angel, take the second floor. Donnie, Gannon, you guys will be on the third floor. Hammer, Gerald, and I will take the top floor." He sounded like a drill sergeant, making eye contact with each of us as he called our name. I cracked a smile. I didn't know if I should salute or laugh, but since I was trying to act more mature, I kept my mouth shut. "Any questions?"

"Hey, Sarge . . ." Hammer chuckled, and the room erupted in laughter.

"I guess I deserved that," Fang replied, giving Hammer a playful shove. "We have some leftover pizza. Help yourself."

Hammer and Gannon wasted no time grabbing a slice. I hesitated, but the smell was overwhelming, so I grabbed a slice for myself. This was some of the best mouthwatering pizza I had ever tasted. I think it was the cheese . . . no, maybe the sauce, or both.

"Thanks." I guess I was hungrier than I thought. Ten, fifteen minutes passed. We gathered our supplies, checked batteries, and went over all the details.

Briskly, we loaded the car, piled in, and huddled to stay warm. The windows fogged over, making visibility impossible. Gabe turned up the heat and then tucked his hand inside his sleeve. Placing his arm on the windshield, he rubbed in a circular motion to clear an area large enough to see through before putting the car into motion. It took a while for the heat to reach us sitting in the back.

I'd watched my mother clean the windshield the same way a hundred times, but tonight seemed different. I wasn't with my mother. I was with my friends, real friends. *It sounds funny when I say it to myself. I have friends.* I felt comfortable, relaxed, something inside told me these guys truly wanted Gannon, Hammer, and me to hang out with them. I should not have doubted them when Sandy made her statement. A smile creased my face as we made our way toward the Blue Owl Inn.

I felt a light tap on my shoulder, and I turned. "You okay?" Hammer grinned.

"I'm excited and looking forward to tonight." A lie, but I didn't want to give away the fact that I was terrified. I'd only been on one ghost hunt and too many things could go wrong. I tensed as the car came to a stop in the parking lot. I inhaled, then cautiously stepped out of the vehicle, zipped my coat up, and braced myself for the long night ahead. It's times like this that I wonder why I'm doing this. But then I remember that I needed to change my life, be accessible, fit in, and be part of the hip crowd. And they say with change comes sacrifice.

A box containing flashlights and one of the cassette recorders were shoved toward me, and I gripped it tight. I glanced around as everyone was making their way to the side door. I fell in line, and this time, I couldn't wait to get inside as the wind ripped through the parking lot.

The door was slightly open. Funny. I thought we had closed that. But then again, the wind was gusty, so it could have blown the door open. I followed behind the others as we entered. I sat my small box with the rest of the supplies in the middle of the floor. Quickly, everyone grabbed their items and set up began. I stuck to Fang and Hammer like glue, still nervous about Lily's warning. My stomach was tangled in knots, yet I forced a smile. Outside, the wind howled, making the building creak and groan. I heard the roar of thunder in the distance. There's nothing worse than a winter thunderstorm.

Fang looked at our supplies and nodded, and then we began the climb. My heart pounded almost as loudly as the creaky boards as I thought of what would be waiting for us upstairs. We cleared the first landing and tackled the next flight of stairs. A cold blast of air rushed downward, pushing us back. "Was that a warning?" I whispered.

"No, it's blowing through the broken windows." Fang sounded sure of himself as he continued the climb. I followed close with Hammer bringing up the rear. The cold air gushed. We paused, then continued. I stumbled but regained my balance. *I'm not stopping until I reach the top.* My fingers shook as I grabbed the railing to steady myself. My breathing slowed, and I did my best to gather my composure. We cleared the final landing, and Fang and Hammer began to set up. I was on the lookout, and I massaged my jawbone and stiffened as I glanced down the hallway. The first door was closed, and I knew the wind didn't do that—someone, something must have shut the door. I moved forward, pausing in the first doorway. I felt something. A wave of panic came over me, as I reached for the handle.

Why am I doing this? It felt like someone was controlling my body. I heard Hammer on the walkie-talkie, requesting

Gabe to hurry to the fourth floor. I cupped the freezing doorknob and jerked my hand away. Something lightly touched my shoulder and I jumped, turning to see it was only Fang. "It's okay. I'm right here."

"I-I can't do this," I stuttered.

"You're doing great, man." He smiled, his voice calm and reassuring.

I heard footsteps behind me, and I knew Gabe had arrived with Dee in tow. A light beam shot past us toward the closed door. Instantly, I noticed the video camera was on. My feet wouldn't move; they felt like they were encased in cement. Slowly the door handle began to turn. I sensed the danger that was about to burst from the door as my mouth fell open with a whimper. "We need to run," I barked.

"I'm here, buddy." Hammer strode to my right. "I'm not going to let anything happen to you."

"It . . . it feels different tonight," I choked out. "Something's wrong."

"Have I ever let anyone hurt you?"

"This isn't someone . . ." I took a deep breath. "This is something."

Fang, Hammer, and I all took a step back as the knob continued to rotate. I fought back the urge to run as I watched in fear. *Why did I think this was a good idea? I'm not brave enough to be a ghost hunter.* I take another step back, and Hammer and Fang follow my lead. The knob slows and stops. *Maybe what's on the other side feels better now that we are backing away? It doesn't want us to enter. After all, we are invading his or her privacy.*

The wait is killing me as minutes pass with nothing happening. Finally, Gabe turned the camera off to save the batteries. More time passes, and I finally sit back on my foldup camping stool. "Did anyone bring any snacks?" Hammer breaks the silence.

"I can't believe you're hungry," I fired back.

"I'm not, just bored, and eating helps pass the time."

An hour has passed, and nothing stirs in the house. I hear my knees rattle from the cold as they begin to shake. Footsteps approach from the rear. I look over my shoulder and see Gannon and Donnie. They whisper something to Fang, but I don't catch it. Thunder growled outside. The storm must be getting close. My heart gave a little kick. Maybe they want to call it a night. I stand and breathe into my hands to warm them. My breath hangs in the air. The temperature has continued to drop. I don't know why, but I called out, "Lily, are you here?"

"It's not like she can leave this place." Gannon chuckled. Hammer and Fang gazed at me.

"I know she can't leave. I just thought if I called out, she might appear."

"It doesn't work like that." Fang swayed back and forth, trying to stay warm.

I sit back on my stool and tuck my fingers under my legs. We'd been here for hours. A few minutes later, Sam and Angel arrive. "Any luck?" Sam asked.

Fang frowned. "I thought for sure they'd show tonight." I can detect the disappointment in his voice.

Hammer paced. "I thought she would show, too."

"Do ghosts get tired?" I asked.

Fang looked baffled by the question. "What do you mean?"

All eyes are on me again. "Maybe they get tired and can only show when they are fully rested. Maybe it drains their power to appear? Does this make sense?"

The silence in the room answered my question—no one had a clue. "Gabe, Dee, can you come to the fourth floor?" Fang spoke on the radio.

Static, nothing but static.

"Do you copy?" Fang barked.

More static, and I started to get nervous. Had something happened to Dee or Gabe? Finally, we heard the word we all needed to hear. "Copy."

Pounding feet approached. Finally, everyone's on the top floor. "It's getting late . . ." Gabe announced.

"I didn't think to bring a watch. How silly was that?" Hammer looked down at his arm. "A little past eleven."

I couldn't believe we've been here for a few hours. "Everyone okay with calling it a night?"

I, for one, was excited to hear those words come out of Fang's mouth. The others seemed to agree. Chatter broke out as we gathered our belongings. We were about to leave when the door at the far end of the hall creaked open and silence fell over us. The door on the opposite side of the hallway opened as well. The entrance lit up as Gabe perched the video camera on his shoulder. Gannon hit the record button on the cassette recorder, and just like that, we were back in business. I was hoping to get out of here, cuddle up in my warm bed, and get the chill out of my bones. But that wasn't going to happen now since we had activity in the corridor.

We watched, and Gabe recorded as the next door swung open, followed by the one on the other side of the hallway. Only two more doors to go, and whatever or whoever was opening the doors would be here. I glanced over my shoulder and noticed everyone's attention was focused on the doors. I wanted to run but remained steadfast. A shiver ran up my spine. The air grew stagnant, and I knew something was about to happen, I could sense it. Electricity warmed my body. There must be some kind of current in the air. I've had that feeling before when they were present—my stomach turned, and my arms and legs went limp. The feeling felt stronger than any I'd ever felt, though. Whatever's coming is more powerful than anything any of us have ever experienced.

"We need to move," I chirped out. "We need to move." I managed to say it louder this time. I watched as another door began to open. "We—" I start to say as the last door handle begins to turn. "We need—" I'm gasping for breath. The final door clicks and starts to swing open. "Run!" I turn toward the stairs, and Hammer and Fang wrap their arms around me.

“It’s okay,” Hammer whispered, his eyes locked on mine. “We’re good.” A tidal wave of cold air barrels down the hallway, toppling us like bowling pins.

“It’s not Lily,” I managed to spit out as I got back to my knees. The others stumbled. Sam and Angel crawled to the stairs. I watched as they broke away out of sight. Dee tugged on Gabe’s arm, trying to persuade him to leave, but Gabe kept the camera rolling. I briefly smiled because I knew we needed to catch as much of this on film as we could. Fang, Hammer, and Gannon stepped in front of me, creating a shield as another wave of cold air sent us back to the floor. I gasped; the wind knocked out of me like I’d been punched in the gut. I managed to get back to my feet and stagger to the broken window, trying to gulp in the fresh air. As the outside air refreshed my senses, I massaged my jawbone, stiffened, and turned around, ready to continue the fight.

I watched as Fang held a wooden cross to protect himself. I flashed back to the days when Hammer and I would watch scary movies at his house. Because Mom forbid me from watching them, I learned enough about the cross to know it only worked on vampires and demons. Now I was hoping I was wrong. I stared down the hallway, my eyes wide with anticipation. Still no sign of Lily or her father. *So, where was the arctic air coming from? Maybe the right question was, who was behind it?* Before I could finish my thought, a door slammed and opened, followed by another. In seconds, all six doors were banging open and closed, and the sound was deafening.

For the first time in my life, I noticed the fear on Hammer's face. I glanced at the stairs, wondering if I should run. I saw Gabe’s camera peeking over the top stair. The dude was smart. He'd taken cover in the stairwell and had enough presence of mind to continue filming.

The temperature plunged, and the slamming and opening of doors continued. Then silence and warmth fell upon us as if someone flicked on a light switch. The air stilled, a calmness I'd never felt before. My mind raced back to something my grandfather once told me about hurricanes—there was always the calm before the storm. We were vulnerable, and I knew it. To heck with Lily, she was on her own, and from what I could tell, we shot enough footage to prove that ghosts lived among us. So why stay any longer and run the risk of getting hurt or even killed?

I was immobilized for a second but found my courage and made a quick dash toward the stairs. "Let's go. We got what we came for." I took cover a few steps down, my eyes peeking over the top step safely tucked behind Gabe. Fang and Hammer hesitated a bit too long. An older man walked out of the doorway and floated toward the guys with a large rifle pointed directly at Fang and Hammer. My heart fell when an ear-piercing bang echoed down the corridor, and I glanced up to see a plume of smoke floating out of the barrel.

The older man laughed as Fang and Hammer stumbled backward. Time stilled, and the boys continued their fall. Fang's arms flailed at his sides, trying to regain his balance. I won't forget the spine-cracking sound he made when he landed flat on his back. Hammer buckled at the knees; his face riddled with pain. Gannon curled himself into the fetal position against the wall.

I was helpless and couldn't move when they needed me the most. Hammer clenched his stomach as his knees buckled on the hardwood floor. The older man loaded another round. I had to do something, or he was going to shoot again. I looked for something to throw, the flashlight I was holding would have to do. A split-second decision may save their lives.

The flashlight flew end over end in the direction of Lily's father. He looked at me as the light passed through him, landing and sliding down the floor. A mouse scurried along the baseboard and ducked behind the door. Lily stepped out into the hallway and let out a piercing scream that made all of us cover our ears. Her father turned to reprimand her, giving us the time we needed. Gabe placed the camera on the step and grabbed the back of Fang's jacket, dragging him to the stairs. The sudden movement startled Fang, and he kicked the floor in a back-peddling motion. "I'm fine, I'm fine," he bellowed.

Hammer raised his hand in front of his face, looked at his palm, then turned his hand over. Much to his surprise and mine, there was no blood. It was beginning to make sense. The gun was part of the older man, so the weapon couldn't be real. Relief engulfed me, and I picked up the camera and pointed it in the direction of Lily and her father. They couldn't hurt us after all. Lily wrapped her arms around her father, and he shoved her to the wall. She tried again, but he was too strong for her. Gannon darted past and bounded down the stairs. I was too preoccupied to realize that Gabe was helping Fang down the stairs until Hammer grabbed my shoulder. "We need to go," he shouted.

"No!" I continued to film.

My body floated upward in one swift motion. I noticed the older man chanting something in my direction. He must have levitated me off the ground. I think he planned to toss me down the stairs. It was at that moment that I realized how wrong I was—ghosts could hurt us. Anxiety washed over me, squeezing the air out of my lungs. I felt a firm grip wrap around my waist as Hammer snatched me up and tossed me over his shoulder. He bolted down the stairs with ease, with me screaming most of the way. He rounded the second-floor landing and continued downward with me bouncing like a sack of dirty laundry. We cleared the final corner and shot down the last flight, dashing through the lobby out the side door into the frigid night air.

Hammer lowered me, my feet touching the gravel, and I knew I was safe. "You little fool," he laughed with relief in his tone, "what were you thinking?"

"I don't know, I just . . . just wanted to make sure we had this on film." I swayed side to side, trying to regain my balance.

"Wow, what a ride! For a second, I thought we were dead." Fang slapped me on the shoulder. "For a geek, you sure are one brave son of a gun." He rubbed my head for good measure.

These were my friends. I was no longer the worm. That was the moment I realized I had become the bird. Hammer cupped his hand around the curve in my neck. "Good job, little buddy."

Pride welled inside. These guys were awesome. The nine of us looked back at the inn. It was quiet, no lights; dormant like when we had arrived. A shiver ran down my neck, making my arms prickle. I couldn't believe it; I was a ghost hunter, and this was a moment I would relish forever.

CHAPTER THIRTEEN

It's been a few weeks since our last ghost hunt, but I still think about that night often. What could we have done differently? I should have embraced Lily's father and asked how we could help. Maybe the results would have been different. Gannon and I hung out with Fang and the boys on the weekends when time allowed. I hadn't heard or seen Hammer since that night, but I knew he'd be back for our next hunt.

When I wasn't attending class or doing homework, I spent most of my free time in the library—reading, studying, and writing about the paranormal. I completed my first manuscript and was working on a second. I felt like I was becoming an expert in the field since I'd seen and talked to ghosts.

Tonight was no different. I was on the third floor in the back of the library when I noticed a white cloud-like object watch me from behind the bookcase out of the corner of my eye. "Hi, Victoria." I smiled as I rose to my feet. "The last time we spoke, you asked me why? Well, I can't answer why you are trapped here, but I might be able to help."

I was nervous, so I shoved my hands into my pockets, mainly because I didn't know what to do with them. "I've learned that ghosts— I'm sorry, I mean spirits like yourself. Can become trapped because of unfinished business. It could be a loved one's missing object or item, but sometimes it has to do with feelings and emotions." I watched as she floated toward me in human form. I could tell I had piqued her interest. “I think you have unresolved feelings. Will you let me help you?” I paused as she gave me a nod. “Close your eyes.” She trusted me and closed her eyes. “Think back to the night when you lost your life. It wasn’t your fault; it was the result of a bad person.” Victoria’s expression had changed. Her face tightened, and I watched as she clenched her fists. “Your anger is holding you here. I need you to let go, forgive him. I know it’s hard, but you can forgive him. I have faith in you.” Her face relaxed a bit and her fists unclenched as her anger eased. “Good, now think about your family and how much you miss them. Wouldn’t you like to see them again?” Her frown turned into a smile. “You’re doing great, Victoria. Would you like to see your mom again? How about your father?” Her smile grew, and I felt calmness surround her. She put off an almost blinding glow. I had the feeling that this might be working. Victoria looked peaceful, happy like I’d never seen before. Her image slowly disintegrated into a thousand small particles—each one twinkling as they drifted away. I watched in silence as only her face remained. Her smile grew brighter and she gazed at me one last time—I think she was trying to thank me—and then she was gone.

I smiled, jumping up and down in silence celebrating my victory. My smile vanished as I gazed at the empty space before me, my emotions all over the place. Did it work? Had I crossed her over? I wanted to scream and shout and tell the world. I placed my hand on the back of the chair and lowered myself down. I couldn’t believe that worked. I was pleased with myself; I was not just a ghost hunter; I was a ghost healer. All the studying had finally paid off. Only one problem remained . . . I had no way to prove it.

Still, I felt like this was a small victory for me and my research. I didn’t know if I should share my story with the rest of the team. Oh, who am I kidding? Of course, I'll tell them. I hope they don't get upset. Oh, here I go again, overthinking things.

I turned my attention back to writing. I scribbled as fast as possible, not wanting to leave any details out. The uninterrupted writing time was right for me. I couldn't believe how quickly the words came. I guess my experiences needed to be documented.

After a restless night of sleep, I readied myself and darted out the door, heading straight to the Pryor Center to visit our literary professor. They said he knew people in the publishing world, and I was interested in his opinion.

I knocked on the door of Professor Wollensak's office.

"Come in," he boomed, threatening to send me scurrying away. I walked into the professor's office and gulped, holding my manuscript tightly. He was a stout little man and looked harmless. He was shorter than I expected and had a receding hairline. I liked his plaid vest, and the bow tie added a nice touch. I could picture myself looking like him twenty years from now.

"Can I help you?"

"Hi, I'm Gerald Dupickle."

His eyes widened as he complimented me on being the youngest student ever to attend the university. I guess my reputation preceded me. "I wrote this manuscript and was wondering if you could take a look?" I handed the pages over. I watched as he thumbed through them, his eyes perking up.

My nerves rattled as the minutes passed. "This is excellent," the professor breathed, "extraordinary!" I beamed with pride as he praised my work, and then he slammed it onto his desk. "What a waste of talent!"

"What?" I stammered, stunned.

"I'm sorry, I didn't mean to scare you, but this isn't a subject you should write about. Why waste your talent on this?"

"Sir, I'm passionate about this subject. Please, if you could just read the manuscript and tell me what you think?" I shot him my sad face, which always worked on Mom.

The professor leaned back in his chair and sighed. "I'll read this," he shook the pages at me, "but I promise you nothing. Do you understand?"

"Yes, sir." With a little luck, maybe he would forward this to his colleague in New York. What more could I have asked for? Chasing the dead wasn't a popular subject. Wow, why didn't I think of that earlier? "Chasing the Dead" . . . that would have made a great book title

* * *

I cherished the weekends, and this one was no different. The extra sleep and knowing all my homework was finished put a smile on my face. I still hadn't shared my experience with Victoria with anyone. I was gazing at the ceiling, wondering when the right time would be, when I was startled by the knock at my door just before Gannon burst in. "Fang wants all of us to watch as a group," he blurted out. My excitement level spiked off the charts. I knew precisely what Gannon was talking about. Finally, the film had been developed and was back from the store. I hated that it took forever, but I understood that these things take time. This was the moment I'd been waiting for, the moment of truth. I couldn't wait to see what we captured on film. My book sales would go through the roof . . . if I had a book. All we needed was tangible proof that ghosts were real.

I only wished Hammer were here to watch this with us. That would make the day extra special for me. I leaned forward and tried to push myself out of bed, but my head spun and I crashed backward.

"Are you alright?"

"Yeah, just excited, I guess."

"I'm happy for you two. Now, if you don't mind, I'm trying to sleep," Kim barked and threw the covers over his head.

"Sorry," we snickered in unison.

"I'll see you in your room after I shower," I whispered. Gannon nodded and closed the door behind him.

I could barely contain my enthusiasm. After cleaning up and getting dressed, I hurried down the hall to Gannon's. He was as ecstatic as me. We strolled over to the Eagles Nest to grab a bite to eat, chit-chatting along the way. I wanted to sit outside on the wall, but winter was in full swing. It was cold, and we had a light dusting of snow covering everything. I'd almost forgotten how pretty things looked in the winter.

Christmas break was around the corner, and I wasn't looking forward to going home. I wanted to stay here and look into some of the other haunted places Fang had mentioned. One place came to mind—an old, abandoned apartment building in the small town of Lamar. It was twelve miles west of the school and in a secluded area. I didn't know much about the place's history, but I couldn't wait to explore the grounds. I needed a good excuse to give Mom why I didn't want, or should I say, couldn't come home for Christmas. First things first, I needed to watch the video with everyone and see what we captured.

Gannon and I finished breakfast and made our way to the library to kill some time. It was the first time I'd noticed the large sign behind the librarian's counter that read, "Lock Haven University— *Where education comes first, and academics soar high!*" I couldn't pull my eyes off the sign. Was I wasting my time trying to prove ghosts exist? I'd come here to get an excellent education and was devoting half my time to chasing ghosts. Even though I'd seen them, talked to them, and felt their coldness, was I doing the right thing?

My grades were high, so it wasn't like I was failing. I knew I had straight A's in all my classes. While finals were around the corner, I wasn't too worried and knew I would make the Dean's List. But, the thought lingered, was I holding back? Could I do more?

However, I had personal goals too, and was chasing my dream. I belonged to a group and surrounded myself with people who cared about me. One goal remained, a girlfriend, which was the only achievement I lacked. I shrugged my shoulders and stared at Gannon.

"What?"

"Nothing," I lied.

"You're acting weird."

"Sorry, I'm—" I stopped mid-sentence, stood, and walked toward the door to greet Hammer as he came strolling through like he owned the place.

"I had a funny feeling you would come, but how did you know?" I thrust my arms out for a hug.

"Back up, dude," he barked as he extended his hand. Shocked, I stepped back and produced my hand to meet his. *When did we start shaking hands?*

Hammer lunged forward, throwing his arms around my body, and tucked my head under his armpit, and began to rub my hair. "Gotcha." He smiled, then released his hold.

"Let go." I squirmed. "I can't believe you're here."

"Well, your eyesight is still good." He chuckled. "I couldn't sleep; the excitement of watching the film kept me awake. I just tossed and turned, and then I noticed the clock read five a.m. So, I decided to get on the road. Oh wait, I almost forgot, your Mom said hi, and by the way, she's looking forward to Christmas break."

Why did he have to ruin it with that comment? "How did you know the film was ready?" I changed the subject.

"Fang called me yesterday, just like he told you, I suppose—"

"He told me," Gannon interrupted, then shook Hammer's hand.

"Good seeing you. Are you staying out of trouble?"

"I've been too busy to get in any trouble; between classes, homework, and studying, that's all I have time for these days. Not to mention, finals start next week, and then we're off for three weeks at Christmas. How are things with you?" Gannon asked.

"Great, nice of someone to ask." I frowned at Hammer's reply.

"Sorry, so . . . what have you been up to?" I asked.

"The new job is going great. They promoted me, so now I'm fixing the cars. I'm a mechanic." Hammer radiated happiness. "A ghost hunting mechanic," he added, swaying back and forth.

It was great seeing Hammer make something of his life. I worried about him and about what he would or wouldn't do with his life. I guess I had nothing to worry about after all. And it hit me—that's what friends do; they care about each other.

"I'm hungry. What's for lunch?" Hammer asked.

We made our way to our seats, picking up food along the way. The afternoon went by slowly. I'm not sure why we always had to wait until dark to meet. Maybe that was Fang's thing. We talked for hours, and before we knew it, we were ready to head over to Fang's. We walked downstairs and Hammer pointed to his ride.

"What, you got a new car?"

"How cool is that?" Gannon danced in delight.

"It's not new, but it rides nice." Hammer flung open the door on his 1957 Chevy two-door coupe. The black cloth seats felt soft and matched the black exterior. I crawled in the back with Gannon sitting up front. Hammer turned the key, and the engine roared to life. I wanted to climb behind the wheel, but I didn't have a license yet. Mom had let me drive a few times, but I never went to take the test.

We rolled down the street, heading toward Fang's apartment. Even though there weren't many students out and about, we still turned a few heads.

The car rolled to a stop, and we climbed out and headed for the stairs. I noticed Gabe's station wagon parked two cars in front of ours. That told me the gang was already here. I felt we were on the cusp of something big. I could barely contain my excitement; I stumbled, and my knee came crashing down on the hardwood surface. Hammer swooped me up and steadied me. "You okay?

"Yes, I'm fine," I growled, feeling annoyed with my clumsy self for missing the step. I limped up to the top level to see the door was already open with Donnie guarding the doorway as Gannon strolled past.

"What's wrong with you, bud?" Donnie asked.

"He doesn't know how to walk." Hammer laughed at my expense.

"I missed the step and banged my knee. But I'll be fine. Thanks for asking." I swallowed my pride and told the truth. That hurt almost as much as the pain in my knee. I gazed about the room; Gabe and Fang were fumbling with a spool of the film on the top post of a giant film projector. I sat in the first empty spot and observed as they wove the movie through the machine's coils, past the light, then out the bottom where they attached the film to the empty spool.

I noticed Angel and Dee hanging a large white sheet along the far wall with clothespins. At first glance, I thought they were doing laundry but quickly realized we needed a blank canvas to project the picture. I felt like I was going to a picture show at the theater. I had been to a few of them, but always with my mother. The girls finished and took their seats. Gannon and Hammer plopped down in the first vacant spot on the floor.

"All set?" Gabe asked as he flicked the light switch off and turned the projector on. The film began to click, click, click, and then rolled along at a steady pace. Black and white images appeared on the sheet. I saw Dee posing for the camera, then Angel showing her bright smile and dancing around. Sam pulled her arm, and they headed up the steps and faded from our view. Donnie and Gannon followed, and I saw myself, Hammer, and Fang ascend the broad staircase. The film went black. We turned to Gabe, who waved a hand, instructing us to relax.

I noticed the back of someone's head. *Oh, it's me.* Hammer and Fang were standing in front of me. The film continued to play. A small flash of light appeared, and some floating specs rolled across the canvas. Fang and Hammer twitched and moved around. We could see down the long hallway where there was an open door. Slowly we observed another door opening. The film zoomed in, the third doorknob turned, and the door swung open. I faintly heard my voice, "We need to move." The final knob turned, and the door swung open. My voice was louder this time. "Run!"

Then I heard Hammer's voice. "It's okay." Then a pause. "We're good." The footage was still showing the empty hallway with the four doors wide open.

A ripple appeared on the screen and rolled down the corridor, sending all of us to the ground like a row of dominos. Something about the image looked fake, almost rehearsed. "It's not Lily," my voice sounded shaky on film as I got back to my feet. We saw Sam and Angel crawl to the stairs. Fang, Hammer, and Gannon stepped in front of me, creating a shield. My excitement level rocketed—we were about to see the older man appear. My knuckles turned white as I gripped the armchair. Another ripple effect dashed across the screen. Those had to be the cold blasts the old man directed at us because we all ended up back on the ground. I watched the footage precariously as I staggered to my feet and headed for the broken window. It looked like I was gasping for air. I turned to face the others, who were now back on their feet.

Fang raised a small wooden cross. The others cast a look at me as I smirked on screen. Everybody could tell I didn't believe the cross would work. Loud bangs rang out as the view changed back to the hallway. All the doors opened and closed randomly. The film zoomed in on Hammer's face, his eyes wide, and he appeared frightened.

Hammer laughed and pointed at the screen. "I wasn't scared."

The doors continued to open and close. "Let's go. We got what we came for." My voice sounded rattled. I moved out of view. Some sort of light beam appeared at the end of the hallway, which cast the illusion of a colorful shadow. That was it, we had proof, and we had captured the image of a ghost on film. My eyes remained glued to the screen. A small smoke cloud appeared in the middle of the hallway, which quickly pushed its way toward Hammer and Fang. We watched as the two buckled at the knees and collapsed to the floor. Another white cloud appeared in front of them, but it didn't take shape. Then a flashlight flew end over end through the air, down the hallway, landed, and skidded across the floor. I'd forgotten I threw the light at Lily's father. Lily's high-pitched scream blared out of the speaker. It hurt almost as much today as it did that night. A hand appeared and grabbed the back of Fang's jacket, dragging him to safety. The film tilted sideways, and we all tilted our heads to the right, trying to catch a glimpse. Finally, the view righted itself, which must have been when I grabbed the camera.

Dee leaned into Gabe's shoulder, Gannon and Fang leaned forward, trying to get a better look at the screen. I gazed back at the screen. Hammer was seen clutching his stomach, then holding his hand in front of his face. A whirl of light danced in the hallway as the flashlights rolled back and forth in a semi-circle. The footage suddenly jerked back and forth and up and down. I knew it was me holding the camera. I recognized my coughing and gagging as I bounced on Hammer's shoulder as we made our way down the stairs. Click, click, and click the film ended, and we watched as the screen went white.

I squinted as Gabe flicked the light switch on. I looked around the room, and much to my surprise, I wasn't the only one with my mouth hanging open. I'm pretty sure they were feeling like I was—excited that we had captured the appearance of a ghost on film. "That was awesome!" I broke the silence.

“What do you mean?” Fang replied. “We got nothing!” He shook his head. “I mean, nothing but a ball of dust, a white blob of light floating in the hallway, along with a few doors opening and closing,” he paused, “all of which could have been done with fishing line and light effects.” He sighed. “No defined image of the old man or Lily, and that’s what we needed.”

“I agree,” Gabe added. “I thought we would be able to see her dad clearly, as we did that night.”

“I don’t understand,” Donnie added. “What happened?”

“There’s only one logical explanation,” Gannon chimed in. “Ghosts can’t be filmed.”

“That’s absurd.” I pointed to the blank sheet hanging from the wall. “The lights were dancing around, the puff of smoke from the gun. Even the doors were moving by themselves.” I took a deep breath. “We have proof. We all saw it. I witnessed it.” I tried to make my case, but no one was buying it, not even Hammer, much to my disappointment.

“So, we are back to square one?” Angel asked, exhausted.

“It sure looks that way,” Sam agreed.

The night hadn’t turned out the way I had hoped. We discussed the topic for over an hour—what we did wrong or may have done wrong, and how we could do things better next time, but without any real solution. I reminded everyone that this was our first attempt using a camera to film something. Maybe we needed a still photo? “So, why didn’t anyone take a Polaroid picture?”

“I guess we were caught up in the moment,” Donnie answered.

“I thought the movie film was going to be all we needed,” Gabe added.

“Next time, we use both,” Fang concluded.

But there was one unanswered question that was nagging me. Why couldn’t we record what we had witnessed with our own eyes? I needed to see what I could find in the library. There had to be an answer to our question in one of the books.

Maybe I should talk to a ghost? But who? Victoria had crossed over, and I wasn’t going back to the inn! We dispersed, heading back to the dorm. Hammer was heading back home tomorrow, and for me, that meant research time at the library.

CHAPTER FOURTEEN

The week was long, with exams and studying. I needed to focus more than I cared to. But after taking the finals, I felt more relaxed and excited about my results. What had happened to the science geek who came to college to learn? I guess he changed, for the better, I hope. I had one more exam, and that wasn't until Tuesday morning—it was math, one of my strongest subjects, which gave me a little free time away from the books. I knew Hammer wasn't coming back to town, and I understood. He couldn't drive into town every weekend, especially on short notice. I convinced Gannon to go to Fang's and see if we could check out the Lamar apartment building he'd mentioned.

A cold arctic blast settled over the valley. Thankfully, Gannon knew a guy who could give us a lift, so we wouldn't have to walk to Fang's apartment on such a frigid day. I wasn't worried about getting a ride back to the dorm. I was sure Gabe wouldn't mind giving us a lift.

It was my last weekend before Christmas break, and I wanted to make fair use of our ghost hunting time. When we arrived at Fang's, I didn't see the station wagon, so maybe Gabe was out running errands. Fang was delighted to see us when he opened his door, ushering us inside quickly. He and Donnie were plotting our next journey.

We took our seats as Donnie opened a notepad and pointed to some notes he had jotted down. "I found this in the archives at the Lock Haven Library. It states the place is haunted by a young man in his early twenties. His name's

William Jacobs. It says he walks the halls at night in search of his pregnant fiancée."

"A pregnant ghost?" I ask.

"I guess so." He stretched his arms. "The article said a team of paranormal experts from New York looked into the story. They visited the site but were not able to prove or disprove the claim," Donnie said.

"That doesn't give us much to go on." Fang added.

"Did you check the old newspaper section?" I blurted out.

"Of course, I did. I've been doing this longer than you." Donnie's nostrils flared.

It wasn't my intention to offend him with my comment. "I didn't mean anything by it." I didn't want Donnie upset with me. "I'm sorry."

"Forget about it. We're cool." Donnie shrugged his shoulders.

"Maybe we'll have better luck than the other team."

"When are we going?" Gannon cut in.

"It would be nice if we knew more about the place and the legend behind why the place is haunted." Fang looked at all of us. "I guess we could do a walkthrough to get a feel." We all nodded our agreement.

"How about today?" I asked anxiously.

Fang nodded. "I'm free."

"Cool," Gannon replied.

Donnie smiled. "So, we're going now?"

"Let's do it." Fang sprang to his feet and grabbed the phone off the wall to call Gabe.

"He'll be here shortly." Fang hung up the phone.

"Hey, um . . . while we're waiting, I . . . ah, kind of helped Victoria cross over." All eyes were on me, yet no one said a word. I rubbed my hands on my knees several times, waiting for a reaction.

"What?" Fang appeared confused. "How? Why?" He stared me down.

"In the library."

"Of course, it was in the library." I detected a hint of frustration in his voice as he spread his arms.

"It just happened. I was reading this article about helping spirits when Victoria showed up. I started talking to her, and one thing led to another . . . Before I knew it, she disintegrated before my eyes."

"Are you kidding me? Tell me you're joking?" Donnie grumbled.

"It's alright," Fang waved a hand at Donnie.

"No, it's not. This cat shows up and starts acting like he owns the place. Fang told you not to get involved, and look at you, crossing over a ghost."

"I'm sorry." I bowed my head out of habit.

“Are you sure she’s gone?” Fang asked.

“I think so, but I can’t be sure. I guess only time will tell.”

“When?” Gannon had been silent until now.

“I don’t know, maybe a week ago.”

“What the heck!” Donnie erupted. “So why didn’t you tell us sooner?” Donnie shook his head at me.

“A week?” Gannon seemed shocked. “Why didn’t you tell us.”

“I don’t know. I wasn’t sure it worked, and I didn’t what you guys getting upset with me.” Gannon and Donnie shook their heads. I explained how everything unfolded that night in the library, not leaving any details out, and they seemed to relax and understand a little better.

Fang eyed me down, and then after a long minute he murmured, “What’s done is done.”

“Just like that, you forgive him?” Donnie eyed Fang, clearly not letting this go.

“I’m truly sorry. It happened so fast, and I didn’t know it would work.” I wobbled back and forth.

“Why hunt ghosts if we can’t help them?” Gannon countered, coming to my rescue.

“We started this group to prove they exist, and we still haven’t done that. I understand you didn’t mean to, but we can’t or shouldn’t get involved. However, you and Gannon make a valid point. Why ghost hunt if we’re not going to help them? We can discuss this more when everyone's here," Fang concluded.

I knew I hadn't won any favor with Donnie. I was thrilled when the knock came at the door. "Burr, it's downright cold out there," Gabe announced with Dee on his heels.

We did our pleasantries, and Gabe pulled out two new cameras from his knapsack. He waved both of them back and forth. "They're loaded with instant-print film. We can use these to get pictures of the layout, or if we see anything." He beamed, proud of all his toys. If I had the money, I would buy one of those cameras for myself, maybe even a cassette recorder, but I didn't have a job and Mom didn't have the money to give me.

I wonder what else he has in his small bag. My thoughts were answered as he pulled out a cassette recorder and three flashlights. "Do we need anything else?"

"I think we're set. Let's go." Fang stood and led the charge.

I grabbed my winter coat. It wasn't as new as the others were wearing, but it kept me warm. I slipped my stocking cap over my head, pulled the gloves from my pocket, and followed the gang downstairs. There was nothing worse than cold ears and frozen fingers.

To my surprise, the car was reasonably warm, but it made sense since Gabe and Dee had just arrived. We drove out of town. I heard the others chatting, but I became lost in my thoughts. Sitting in the backseat made my stomach a little uneasy as we sped up and down the rolling hills of the old country road. This was the farthest I'd been away from the campus since I arrived, which made this trip special, not to mention this was the first time I'd ventured out in the daylight. I couldn't help but notice the long rows of corn or hayfields covered in a fresh blanket of snow. Cow pastures, red wooden barns, and silos dotted the landscape. The scene was breathtaking.

I noticed Gannon glance at me a few times. *I wonder if I hurt his feelings by not telling him about Victoria. I'll apologize to him later for keeping this to myself for so long.*

The car slowed as we rolled into the small town of Lamar. I noticed one red light blinking in the middle of town—a gas station on the corner, a family restaurant next to that. A small wood-framed building followed. There wasn't much here. I wasn't sure what I had expected, but it was only a fraction of the size of the town where I grew up. Fang had told us the town was small. The main attraction was the National Fish Hatchery, which was down the road from the apartment building. Fang said the hatchery had cottages that skirted the banks of Big Fishing Creek and mentioned the lodge even used to house the inner-city kids in the summer months. They came here to learn about fishing and hunting, experiences they couldn't get in the city. The town flourished when the place was built, but over time, it declined. The jobs never came, and things dried up rather quickly. All that remained were a few stores and a scattering of houses.

I noticed a blinking *We're Open* sign in the front door of Uncle Bob's Hoagies. I must have caught a whiff of the hoagies because I was hungry all of a sudden. Gabe mentioned we should stop on the way back because they had great-tasting sandwiches and the bread was always warm. My hand slid into my pocket, knowing I didn't have enough to buy lunch.

“Don’t worry, I’ll cover you.” Gannon nudged me. Having friends was the best thing about college.

“Thanks!” I bowed.

Gabe turned on his left blinker as we turned. We didn’t travel far before turning down an old dirt road. I noticed a Victorian-style three-story building sitting in the overgrown field of brush and tangled thicket of trees covered with snow. It didn’t look like anyone had been here in years. The faded paint peeling off the sign read ‘L mar Apa t ents.’ The place and sign had seen better days for sure, but all the windows seemed to be intact, which was a plus because it would be warmer inside.

The brakes squealed and the car jerked to a halt. We sat and admired the beauty of the place. I imagined what it would have been like back in its glory days—the hustle and bustle of people coming and going . . . children playing kickball in the vacant field next to the building or even exploring the pine forest located on the property's left side.

“Are we ready?” Fang interrupted my thoughts.

Car doors swung open, and we quickly made our way to the front doors. I didn’t notice any chains or locks and the door swung open with ease. The smell of rotten carpet and mildew engulfed me as we stopped just inside the entryway. *Don’t throw up, don’t throw up.* Now was not the time for that. With a little luck, I was able to keep my breakfast down. The lobby was small, nothing fancy at all. Everything was connected to a long hallway, with doors on each side. It almost resembled the Blue Owl Inn, but it wasn’t as elegant.

I became anxious, and I couldn't wait to explore the place. Gabe opened his bag and handed Fang a flashlight. I wasn't sure we would need them, but it was better to be safe than sorry, I guess. He gave one to Gannon, and he kept the last one for himself. He handed Dee one of the cameras and the other to me. "Do you know how to use it?" I nodded. "If you see something strange, point and press." He pointed at the black button on the front of the camera.

"Let's stick together," Fang suggested and motioned for us to follow. Donnie stayed glued to Fang's side; Gabe and Dee walked side by side, bringing up the middle, while Gannon and I brought up the rear. One by one, we stopped at the first door on the right. The opening was double the standard door's size, and I realized it was an elevator shaft. I looked up at the dark space, and I glanced down to more of the same. The shaft was empty, and that gave me a creepy vibe. What happened to the carriage or cage that would have carried people between the floors? For some reason, I found that interesting.

"Be careful." Fang placed his arm before me, ushering me back.

"I wonder why it was removed." Gannon whispered.

We journeyed farther down the hall. Fang pushed each door open and peeked inside, then moved on to the next. Donnie stepped into each room to get a better look before proceeding. Like puppets on a string, we all peeked our heads in for a few seconds. Most of the places were empty. One had an old broken-down bedframe while another contained a small child's desk. It reminded me of the kind you would see in elementary school. I noticed each room had a small fireplace, which I guess was the only source of heat.

Fang turned right at the end of the hallway, disappearing around the corner. I heard the wood creaking underfoot. "It doesn't smell as bad now," I said, but kept my voice low.

"Most of the carpets have been removed," Gannon noted as he shined the light toward the floor. I nodded and picked up my pace to catch up with the group.

I turned the corner and stepped on the first board. I heard it crack and quickly pulled back. "It's fine," Gabe whispered, "Come on." He turned, continuing down the corridor.

Something was off. I couldn't put my finger on it. A warm, calm stillness hung in the air, and an eerie feeling vibrated through me. Something was about to happen; I could feel it. Gannon nudged me in the back. "Let's go."

We trekked up a few more stairs. The others were already halfway down the second-floor hall as we turned the corner. I fumbled with my steps but strode forward, trying to catch up. Fang waved a hand behind him and I stopped dead in my tracks. "Did he see something?" I whispered, my voice sounding weary.

"I don't know," Dee replied.

We stood motionless for a few seconds, my heart thumping in my chest. Moments passed, and cautiously, we continued to the end of the hall and around the corner, making our way to the next flight of stairs. There were two exits on each floor—the stairs and the empty elevator shaft. I quivered at the thought. There had to be another way in and out. Perhaps I missed something. Maybe there was another staircase on the backside of the building.

A shiver ran down my spine, but it wasn't from the cold. There was something here. I could feel it, like an extra sense that I possessed. "Tell them we're close." I steadied my voice, giving Dee and Gabe a meaningful look. The message echoed forward.

With my gaze intent as I peeked through an open door, another vacant room greeted me. I glided along to the last entry. The others were already making their way up the final flight of stairs. I scuttled back, then looked again. It was a red tricycle, but it didn't look like it was abandoned—it looked new. I suppressed a shiver, my upper lip curling automatically, and I bit my lip to stop the face I was making. I'm not sure why, but this bike had me perplexed. *Could someone be living here? A child, perhaps? A mother and a child? A family?* I jumped as Gannon tapped my shoulder.

"Don't do that," I whimpered, my heart pounding.

"Sorry." He stepped past me and started climbing the stairs.

I snapped out of my stupor. I was alone. I took a final look at the bike, then turned, wanting to catch up with Gannon. I scurried onto the top of the stairs, gazing down the hallway to the far end. Excitement surged through my veins, and my pulse pounded in my ears. The feeling that something was about to happen had me on edge. I noticed a huge gap between myself and the others. I stepped back slightly and realized my foot was in midair. I reached forward to regain my balance, but it was too late, and with a cry, I fell, tumbling down the stairs as every step threw a punch at my head and gut.

I gasped for breath as the floor slammed into my back and I fought for the air that fled from my lungs. I laid there, staring at the ceiling as my breath slowly returned. Thankfully, I was bundled up for winter, so my heavy clothing protected my back during my fall. It seemed I was only battered and slightly bruised, not to mention, embarrassed—at least I didn't notice any blood. A breath of warm air rolled down the back of my neck, I opened my eyes, but there was no one there. "I'm sorry," a voice whispered in my ear. I looked right, then left, and quickly stumbled to my feet. I caught a glimpse of a girl running away. She stopped, looked back, and our eyes connected. I was speechless. She seemed to be around my age, but why would she be here? Was she a local girl? Her sneakers looked rough, her jeans dirty, and her jacket was torn. She frowned before heading down the stairs.

"Wait," I cried.

I was ready to pursue her when firm hands tugged at my shoulder.

"You alright?" Fang asked.

"Yes," I managed to get out and tried to move forward away from the wall, but Donnie pinned me fast.

"You okay? Look at me, Gerald!" He was holding up two fingers.

"Two," I blurted out. I noticed Dee's smile over his shoulder.

"Sorry, I missed the step and lost my balance, but I'm alright," I assured them.

We hiked back upstairs, my knee a little sore. Everyone stayed close to me. I felt a little idiotic; I've always been clumsy, and now that they had noticed my clumsiness, they were pampering me.

We gazed inside each room. Most of the places were empty, but one room caught my attention. The fireplace contained a pile of ashes. A child-sized mattress was tucked in the corner, with a pillow and blanket, along with an old suitcase nestled inside the open closet. I couldn't help but wonder if that girl was living here. I dismissed my findings and nodded for us to leave.

We moseyed our way downstairs, glancing in a room or two along the way. Fang and Donnie were discussing whether we should come back that evening for a ghost hunt. I felt they were right. This would be the perfect location for a spirit to live. *But what if we find the girl? Then what?* My heart fluttered.

I looked in a few more rooms. *Where could she hide?* Fang, Donnie, and the others were ready to skedaddle when I raised the issue. "What about the basement?"

"Great idea," Donnie responded. "Fang and I will check it out and meet you in the car."

I had meant for me to look downstairs, but I didn't want to create suspicion, so I played along as we made our way to the car. I groaned a little as I sat in the cushioned seat, my spine slightly tender.

Moments later, the car doors swung open, and Fang and Donnie bounced in. "The basement was empty," Donnie rattled off before the car lunged forward.

I'm not sure why, but I didn't mention the girl to anyone. Maybe it was the brief eye contact we shared or her golden hair blowing in the breeze as she dashed out of sight. Or perhaps it was because she looked real and not like a ghost.

CHAPTER FIFTEEN

We assembled our group later that evening, and the drive to the Lamar Apartments looked much different at twilight. Cloudy skies blocked any chance of seeing the sunset. I wasn't sure, but by the way the trees swayed in the breeze, we might be in for a winter storm. Maybe that's why Fang decided to leave earlier than usual.

The car turned down the short gravel lane, and the apartments were coming into view. I peered out the window, looking for any light seeping from the windows. Then it hit me. If she were homeless, she would have found a room on the building's backside so no one would see the light. She was smart and elusive; that's how she survived out here. I liked that.

"Gerald, are you coming?"

"Ah, yeah," I hadn't even realized the car had stopped, and both girls, along with the guys, were already out of the vehicle. The bitter cold air slapped me in the face as I stepped out. I quickly pulled my stocking hat down over my ears and trotted toward the front door.

The groups were a little different this evening. Gabe and Dee were setting up in the basement. Sam and Angel remained on the first floor, and Donnie and Gannon perched out on the second. Fang toted the flashlight while I held the camera, and we slowly proceeded up the stairs as we headed to the third floor. In a way, I felt sorry for Sam and Angel. They were always holed up on the first floor away from all the action, but maybe they liked it that way.

We pulled out our camp stools and perched ourselves at the top of the stairs. The first hour slipped away quickly. We rubbed our hands over and over, trying to keep them warm. I informed Fang that I wasn't getting any weird vibes tonight. As I mentioned it, I wondered if Fang could explain why I got those feelings. After a bit of hesitation, I asked, "Why do I attract ghosts?"

"I'm not exactly sure." Fang fiddled with his hands. "I think it has to do with your IQ level. Your brain works differently than most people. I think you can tune into them, and maybe they can sense that."

"Well, I can't argue with that. I mean, I'm a genius." I scratched my itching palm.

"One-point shy, if memory serves me correctly."

We shared a laugh and enjoyed our one-on-one time. It was the first time Fang and I had a chance to talk like this. In fact, it was the first time I had ever been along with Fang. He was intelligent and knew a lot about history, not to mention he was a pretty cool dude. We swapped stories and shared idle chit-chat for the next hour. Then Fang decided to try a different approach.

"William . . ." Fang spoke softly. "William, are you here? We're here to help if you can hear us."

"What are you doing?" I whispered.

"Sometimes ghosts respond when you talk to them. That's what we did before you came along."

"Does it work?"

“Not really,” he smiled and shrugged, “but it makes me feel like I’m trying.”

I snickered, then screams and shouting erupted downstairs. It was one of the girls. I hoped everything was alright. Fang and I bounced to our feet and pounded down the stairs. Donnie and Gannon were just ahead of us. Angel was in a hysterical state, her arms flailing around and screaming. Sam was bent over laughing. Dee ran in and tried to comfort Angel, with little to no luck. I looked around, but I didn’t see anything out of the ordinary. What could have set Angel off?

“What’s going on? Did you see something?” The words slipped out harsher than Fang must have intended.

“No, no,” Sam repeated, trying to catch his breath.

“Will someone please tell us what’s going on?” Fang pleaded in a strained tone.

“Raccoon,” Sam spat out. “It was a raccoon, it appeared over there.” He pointed toward the basement door. “Its beady little eyes shined in the light, and when it squealed, Angel screamed, and the poor guy took off.” He continued to laugh.

I chuckled under my breath, and I noticed the others doing the same. “You . . . you should have seen her reaction,” Sam stuttered, trying to regain his composure.

“It wasn’t funny. The damn thing scared the crap out of me!” Angel paused. “You all are a bunch of jerks.” Angel laughed and then scolded us as she paced back and forth.

Sam embraced her. “That’s my girl.”

We waited for things to calm down. We had been here for hours, and the only action we'd seen or heard was from a raccoon. Was the place haunted? Or was it just a dead end? The wind howled outside, and the air was much colder down here on the main floor. Everyone was ready to pack it in. Fang asked me to get the stools as he handed me the flashlight, so I headed back upstairs. When I cleared the second-floor landing, a weird feeling rushed over my body. My heart galloped, and I stumbled onward. I just needed to grab the chairs and get out of here. My toes and ears were cold, and I was ready to head back to the dorm where it was warm and toasty.

I was startled by a creaking sound on the floor above. I froze in my tracks, cocking an eyebrow. "Is anyone there?" My voice sounded tight. I could sense I was not alone. Was it the girl? If it was, where had she been hiding? Fang and I had checked all the rooms when we first arrived. I took another step, then two. I gazed over the landing and down the hallway. "Is anyone here?" I asked firmly. "I'm here to help."

Moments passed and nothing happened, not even a sound. I took another step with only the creak of the floorboards underfoot. I poked my head in the first room, nothing. I glanced around the corner in the second, which was also empty. I was nervous about going any farther down the hall. *I should grab the chairs and get out while I can.* My inner sense told me we came here to find a spirit, but I wasn't sure what I was looking for. Was there really a ghost or was I hoping to run into the girl from this afternoon?

I stepped closer, pushing open another door. Once again, the room was empty. I felt silly, and I knew I was wasting my time. The wind outside howled. *The storm must be getting close. We should head back to the dorms before the weather turns*. The wall creaked, and I glanced in that direction. I was pretty sure that was the sound I heard. Plus, I knew if I stayed up here any longer, the others would come looking. *Wouldn't they?* I started to doubt myself. *Would they?* I shook my head in frustration. What was wrong with me? Of course, they would search for me. A noise echoed down the hall and I snapped to attention.

With my mouth agape and panic flooding my body, I walked back into the hall. There were only three rooms left. The sound had to be coming from the room with the mattress. "I'm not going to hurt you." I stumbled on my words and took a deep breath, steadying my voice. "Please let me help." My breathing was shallow and quick. My heart was about to leap out of my chest. I needed to be brave. I needed to stay calm.

I noticed fingers wrap around the last doorway. I froze in my tracks only a few feet away from the door. Slowly the girl appeared. I saw wavy blonde hair cascading past her shoulders. There was a softness in her hazel-colored eyes, and she looked nervous. "Hi." I gave a slight wave. She blinked a few times, so I shined my light toward the floor as not to blind her. She could not have been much older than me. Her skin resembled a porcelain doll. Her cheeks pinked and appeared soft. She stood on the threshold. She was a bit shorter than me, wearing a pair of old blue jeans and a pale pink T-shirt, covered with an old plaid flannel long-sleeved shirt. I couldn't help but notice the pink sock showing through the hole in her left shoe. She was picture-perfect. *Where are my manners?* "Are you cold?" She glared at me. Her lips parted like she wanted to say something.

“Are you hungry?” I asked, immediately feeling idiotic, knowing I didn’t have any food to offer. She softly tilted her head to one side, checking me out as I had done to her. I let her exam me top to bottom before I spoke again. “I mean you no harm.” I wanted to know her better, and I wanted her to leave this awful empty place. It must have been so lonely living here.

Her mouth wrinkled as if she wasn’t quite sure how to respond. Her hand moved to her hair, and she twirled a strand around her finger a time or two. Was she flirting with me? I had no experience in this area, so I wasn’t sure how to respond. I could see every breath I took in the night air. I wanted to shine the flashlight directly at her, but that could frighten her away.

I cleared my throat. “I’m Gerald,” I said, my voice raspy. Her lips parted, then closed. I could tell she wanted to say something, but she must be terrified facing an unknown enemy in her own house. “I’m not going to hurt you, I promise.”

“I’m Leela.” Her voice sounded sweet on my ears.

“Did you say, Leela?”

“Yes,” she mouthed the word.

A creaking noise echoed behind me. I turned and noticed a beam of light dancing in the stairwell. I held my palm before me. “What’s taking so long?” Gannon asked.

“Quiet.” I pointed behind me.

Gannon flashed his light behind me.

“Stop.”

“What?”

I turned, puzzled, and gazed down the empty hallway. It didn’t surprise me that Leela had taken cover. She must have ducked back into her room. “There’s a girl—” I didn’t finish; I only pointed to the room as panic deepened my senses. I’m not sure why I felt the need to share that information. I certainly didn’t want to blow her cover. I wasn’t sure how others would react. My eyes stayed sharp as Gannon walked to the end of the hall, beams of lights crisscrossing back and forth as he scanned the vacant room. I peeked over his shoulder, and I’m not sure why, but Gannon walked to the closet. I knew he had found her hiding spot. “Nothing here.” Gannon nodded.

I was shocked to see the space empty. The dirty suitcase laid closed on the floor next to the mattress. Part of me wanted to open it, but my conscience told me that it was not the right thing to do. Why was I pushing to prove I had seen a girl? I guess I didn’t want them to think I had lost my mind.

“There’s no one here, just an old play mattress and case, I’m sure it’s something the local kids left behind,” Gannon said sharply. “Are you alright, Gerald?”

I looked at him, wanting to defend my stance, but my heart softened. “Maybe it was your light coming up the stairs that I noticed.”

“You thought my light was a girl?”

“No, I mean, it was like a reflection.” I felt foolish lying to Gannon, but I wanted to protect Leela, even though I had only seen her twice. I knew right then that I needed to call Hammer and have him drive me back here so I could bring her some food and gain her trust.

"Maybe you did, or maybe you didn't see anything. But I'm hungry, so grab a chair and let's get out of here." I watched as he grabbed one of the stools and trotted down the stairs. I lagged for a second, turning to look over my shoulder. "I'll be back," I whispered. "I'll bring you some food and a blanket. I promise." I spun around and grabbed the chair, then slowly proceeded toward the others.

I stopped at the top of the first-floor landing. I noticed everyone was staring at me. I wondered what was going through their minds as I approached. "What?" I hollered.

"Did you see something?" Fang questioned.

"I'm not sure,"

"Don't lie to me," Fang fired back. "No more secrets dude, we have to trust each other."

I nodded and caved under pressure. "It might have been a girl, but she's gone."

"What do you mean, a girl?" Sam asked.

"Like a homeless person."

"Man, nobody lives here."

"Are you sure about that?"

"Yes, positive." Sam seemed sure of himself, though I wasn't sold on that theory.

“Okay, then, that’s settled.” Sam rolled his eyes at me. “Do we need to go upstairs and search the upper floor to prove it?” I could tell I had touched a nerve with Sam.

“No, we're good.” I nodded. “Gannon and I looked, and as I told him, it must have been a reflection of the light or something to that effect.”

“Great, it’s settled then,” Fang interrupted. “The last one in the car is a rotten egg.” Everyone disappeared in a flash, leaving Gannon and me to wonder what happened.

“I guess we’re the rotten eggs.” Gannon and I shared a laugh as we strolled toward the car.

CHAPTER SIXTEEN

Finals were over, and I was confident I had aced all my tests. It was Christmas break, and the campus was pretty sparse. I had lied to my Mom and told her Professor Ream was conducting chemistry experiments and requested a few honor students to join him. She fell for my lie; it wasn't my proudest moment, and I was sure it was going to come back to haunt me. I do love and miss my mom, but three weeks with her was a bit much. Especially when I had so much to do. So, I conceded and agreed to let Hammer drive into town and bring me home for a few days. Sometimes we have to do the right thing to please our parents, even if it's not what we had planned.

I sat on the edge of my bed, tapping my feet against the floor. With Kim gone for the holidays, I had the entire room to myself. I debated on getting some breakfast or waiting to have an early lunch. Either way, I would be eating alone—something I hadn't done since college started. With Gannon and most of the ghost hunters on holiday break, except for Fang and Gabe, I found myself with plenty of free time. However much free time I had, there was still one thing I needed to do, and that was help Leela. *I only lacked the mode of transportation to see her. She's probably wondering why I haven't returned as promised.*

If I could only swing by the local grocery store and grab a few things, I could brighten Leela's day. I counted the cash I had tucked away in my luggage—it wasn't much, but two dollars was better than nothing. I was sure Mom would give me some cash for Christmas, so I didn't mind spending what

I had left on Leela. My next challenge was to convince Hammer to drive me to the apartment building when he arrived. *I can't stand to see her go hungry over Christmas.* The thought of Christmas put my mind in overdrive. *Did she even know what time of the year it was, other than winter? Did she know it was Christmas? Did she even care?*

I felt sorry for her, being alone all the time, trying to survive in this cruel world by herself. What happened to her family? Were they still alive? If they were, how could they abandon their daughter? *Oh, my goodness, if I don't stop thinking about this, I'll give myself a massive headache.* I needed to do some research . . . that always solved everything. But that created another problem. How do I research a homeless person without knowing her last name? Even if I had that information, I would still need to find a newspaper article containing the information I sought. What if there were no missing person reports? Or an article about a family killed in a car crash, survived by their sixteen-year-old daughter who was now homeless?

Man, I needed to talk to Leela. My feelings were genuine. I truly wanted to help, maybe even give her a real place to stay. My mom could use some help around the house, but we were poor and couldn't pay her. Maybe she could work off the rent money. *Oh, I don't know.*

I felt trapped and didn't exactly know how to solve this situation. I was one-point shy of being a genius, so why couldn't I figure this out? Frustration overwhelmed me. Then I remembered something Hammer once told me. Yes, Bates, the not-so-bright kid who now had a good job and owned a car. The last time I spoke with him, he even mentioned renting an apartment.

But I could remember that day in the driveway clearly. I must have been twelve or thirteen years old. He said, "You need to take baby steps. You can't learn to walk in a day, so take steps. Solve one problem, then the next."

That was it.

That's what I need to do, take steps or action. That meant planning. The first thing I needed to do was take some food to Leela—that's if she hadn't moved away. After all, her living quarters had been compromised. But why would she run in the middle of winter? *Don't overthink this. Stop, think. Step one, I'll take her some food. Step two, I will earn her trust, and maybe she will answer some of my questions. Step three, I will research until I know her story, unless she tells me everything I need to know. Step four, help her find a place to live and finally, help her land a job.*

Now that I had everything worked out in my head, I just needed to execute it. I frowned. I couldn't do anything myself. I've always had to rely on someone. There was a sudden knock on the door. Startled, I bounded to my feet. Everyone was gone, so who could it be? It couldn't be Hammer. I knew he wouldn't arrive until Monday. I hurried to the door, excited that Hammer must have arrived early to surprise me and flung the door open. My smile quickly vanished. "Professor Wollensak." I almost didn't recognize him in his blue jeans and leather jacket.

"Hello, Gerald." He smiled. "May I come in?"

"Sure," I stepped aside. I was embarrassed, still being in my pajamas, and my room not as tidy as one would expect. "Would you like to sit?" I pointed to Kim's bed.

"Thanks." He sat down, though he seemed uncomfortable.

I noticed a folder in his hand. "Is everything alright?" I was puzzled as to why the literary professor would visit my room.

The professor furrowed his brow. "I'm glad I caught you before Christmas." He pushed the folder toward me. "My colleague in New York liked your manuscript so much that he called his editor friend, who works for a large publishing company in the city. They both agreed. They loved your story."

I opened the folder and found a contract from Viking Publishing. Wide-eyed, I gazed at the papers in my hand—the same publisher who signed Arthur Miller, who wrote *Death of a Salesman* and *The Crucible*. I'd read his work and loved it. They were offering me money to publish my story. I started reading every line, occasionally glancing up at the professor, then back to the papers in hand. My hands began to tremble, my throat became raw; it was hard to breathe, hard to speak. I couldn't believe this was happening to me. I turned to the final page and attached was a check made out to me. Flustered, I let the documents fall to the floor. "Oh my gosh, oh my, there must be a mistake."

"My boy, it's no mistake." Professor Wollensak smiled at me. "You're only the second student to be published from our school. You should be proud."

I was more than proud. I was beaming. The publisher had suggested changing the title to "Defeating Dark Entities." I wasn't fond of that, but I glanced at the check again. How could I refuse a check for $1,000, especially when the minimum wage was only $1.62 an hour? “Yes,” I mumbled under my breath.

“What’s that?” Professor Wollensak asked.

“I don’t understand this line. This contract is for a fictional story. I’d written about my life events.”

“Gerald, ghost stories are fiction,” Wollensak paused, and his knee began to twitch.

“But I’ve seen and talked to them.” I gazed at the professor, trying to plead my case. Then I remembered something Fang had mentioned. We had no proof. I paused. *I really could use the money.* I needed to swallow my pride. “So, where do I sign?”

He smiled and pointed at me like I was playing a joke on him. “I thought you’d be happier.” He appeared displeased with my reaction.

“I’m . . . I’m just in shock,” I lied.

“Let me explain,” he continued. “They’re offering you a three-book deal. You will need to write two more books. One thousand dollars upfront for each story you submit, and another $1,000 for each book when they release. Plus, royalties. Six thousand over the next three years, that’s not counting royalties. It’s all explained in the contract. Oh, before I forget. I’ll be representing you since you came to me. Is that alright?”

“I don’t know what to say.”

"Say yes, take the check, and sign the contract. Then you'll need to sign the consent form allowing me to represent you."

I was at a loss for words. I was about to become a published author at the age of sixteen. Professor Wollensak handed me a dark blue pen. I admired the Viking logo on the side of the ink pen. I gripped it firmly and signed the agreement, then placed the check on the bed next to me.

"I suggest you put that in a safe place until Monday. If you like, I can take you to the bank and help you open an account. Then you can write me a check for my portion."

"What do you mean?"

"I get fifteen percent for my services. It's customary."

I glanced up at the professor and nodded. I didn't know much about contracts, but it only seemed fair. "Thank you." A tear tracked down my cheek. Today was by far the happiest day of my life. "Monday morning is perfect." I lunged forward and gave him an awkward hug. To my surprise, he hugged me back.

"Now you better get to work on another story. We have a six-month deadline." He handed me a twenty-dollar bill.

"What's this for?"

"It's an advance so you can celebrate a little. Pay me back Monday." We both smiled.

"Thank you, and the deadline is no problem." Little did he know, I had already written the next story. I only needed to tweak a few things, and I could turn the manuscript over to him. I also had an idea for a third book. I just couldn't believe they were publishing my story.

I was delirious and danced around the room like a lunatic after the professor left. All my problems were solved. It was a dream come true. Who says good things don't happen to good people?

My mind whirled with what to do with the money. I would buy a used car. I could put some money into savings, and I would give my mother a hundred dollars. Maybe keep a hundred to live on for the rest of the school year. I knew I wanted to pay back Gannon for his generosity. I also owed the professor his cut for being my representative. This was the break I needed. I held my palm out and looked at the twenty in hand. I might even be able to spend a little extra on Leela.

I needed to share the news with my mother but decided to wait to see her expression in person. I knew she would be as excited as I was. Oh, the waiting was killing me! I had to tell someone! I was never good at keeping secrets. I knew the minute Hammer arrived I would blab to him, and for the first time, I could buy him lunch and offer some gas money. There were so many things I wanted to do with this money. I couldn't believe this was happening to me, all over a few words scribbled on paper.

CHAPTER SEVENTEEN

I grabbed my coat, hat, and gloves and made my way toward the Eagles Nest for lunch. The frigid air cut like a knife, but my heart was filled with warmth from the news I'd received. I snatched a bite to eat and decided to walk into town. Maybe I'd buy a new pair of jeans and a shirt so I could impress my mother over Christmas. Now I was excited to go home. Oh! I had a better idea. I could finally buy her the gift I had always wanted to get her! And what if I bought Mom a card and gave her a hundred dollars? She could buy whatever she wanted for Christmas. Not to mention, she couldn't refuse a Christmas gift. I grinned as a car pulled up in the street. "Gerald!" I looked to my right, and much to my surprise, it was Gabe. "Get in," he hollered.

I didn't think twice. I dashed over, flung the door open, and slid into the front seat. "Shotgun," I called.

"There's no one else here." He cackled with a grin. "But sure, you can call shotgun." Gabe shot me a sidelong glare. "Where were you heading?" he asked, putting the car into motion.

"I was just walking and thinking." I paused.

"Well, I'm heading over to Fang's. Wanna go?"

"Sure." We exchanged some idle chitchat on the drive over, but I wanted to save the big news for both of them. A few moments later, we turned down the alley and parked the car. I leaped out of the car and bounced up the steps like I was floating on air. Fang was putting away dishes as we burst through the door, and he looked excited to see us. "Sorry, you just missed breakfast."

"I ate on campus."

"Dang, late again," Gabe added.

Fang turned and looked at me, where I was bouncing on my toes. "Why are you so giddy? Hope you don't think I bought you a Christmas gift?"

I smiled. "No, and I didn't buy you a gift, either," I jabbed back. Then I proceeded to share my colossal news. At first, they both appeared stunned by the news, but then Fang wrapped me in a giant hug.

"I didn't even know you were writing a story about ghost hunting. That's awesome." Fang couldn't contain the smile that spread on his face.

"Fantastic, now you can buy the next camera." Gabe laughed and patted me on the back. "Great job."

I mentioned we should change the name of the team to something cool. I suggested either The Ghosts Exterminators or The Eagle Paranormal Squad because I wanted to mention the team and everyone's name in the book's acknowledgments. They both seemed thrilled by the idea.

This was the kind of day I had always dreamed about. I felt accomplished. And my friends were excited for me—there was nothing fake about it. They beamed with pride, glad to be in my presence, and my confidence soared.

Fang changed the subject, talking about an old axe factory in Mill Hall located only five or six miles away. He said they used to make tools around the turn of the century. The place was supposed to be haunted; some of the workers had vanished, and there was even an unsolved murder on the property. I was intrigued.

"When do we go?" I asked, my voice eager.

"Slow down. We should wait for everyone to come back from Christmas break. There's safety in numbers, you know."

I totally forgot we were off for the next three weeks and wondered why he was determined to wait. Fang, of course, was right. I snarled a bit but didn't let that dampen my mood. I mentioned Hammer would arrive soon, which would give us another body, but they were adamant about waiting until everyone was back from Christmas break.

Gabe, Fang, and I spent the rest of the afternoon looking at old photos and listening to previous recordings. We even watched the Blue Owl footage again to make sure we hadn't missed anything.

After saying goodbye to Fang and hitching a ride back to the dorm with Gabe, I thanked him for the evening as I slid from the worn leather seat to the brick street. It had been a great afternoon, but now I had work to do. I ran back to my room and grabbed my knapsack before heading to the library. If the group didn't want to go on a ghost hunt, then maybe I could confirm Victoria had crossed over to the other side. That was the best I could hope for tonight.

I entered, going straight to the third floor. I took my favorite seat in the rear, opened my notepad, and began writing. I worked on my story as the hours passed.

"Excuse me, have you noticed the time?" a woman demanded.

Shocked, I glanced up to see the librarian pointing at her watch. I'd forgotten they closed early over the holidays. I gazed at the clock on the wall, it was ten p.m., and I realized I'd missed dinner. I packed up and left with mixed emotions. There wasn't anything unusual or eerie feeling in the air. Maybe that meant Victoria was gone. It gave me hope that she may have crossed over. I thought about that as I returned to my dorm with my stomach growling. My only other regret was not getting my Christmas shopping done.

I pushed the door open to the silence of my room. *Dorm Sweet Dorm*. I was glad to be out of the arctic air. I hadn't realized how cold it was until my bones started to hurt all over my body. I grabbed a bag of chips from my dresser and a soda off the window ledge, thankful that it wasn't frozen, and figured that should at least curb my appetite. Then I cleaned up my mess as I prepared to hit the sack. I bounced into bed and pulled the covers up to my neck to warm my soul. I grabbed a book from my nightstand, turned the pages as I tried to read, but nodded off to another world.

* * *

I snorted and woke myself—a beam of light shining through the curtains. For a moment, I thought someone was shining a light in my window, but much to my surprise, it was morning. My tummy growled, and I knew the first thing I needed to do was eat. I readied myself, grabbed my coat, hat, and gloves, and flung the door open. "Oh crap," I yelled and jumped away from the door.

Hammer busted out laughing, dropped his bag, and hugged me. "You startled me, too," he admitted. Hammer was early, which was becoming a habit—one I liked. He pushed his bag into my room, and we strolled down the hall as I shared the great news with him. He was encouraged that my story was being published. When he asked about the money, I explained I was a first-time author, and they didn't offer me much, not telling him the total amount. One thing my mother always told me was never to discuss your finances with anyone except family. We hopped into Hammer's car and drove to the Eagles Nest. His ride was sportier than the station wagon Gabe owned and was warmer than walking.

On the way, my thoughts returned to Leela, and I wondered how she was fairing in such blistering cold. The knowledge of her fighting for her life alone weighed down on me, and I glanced over at Hammer as he steered the car down the street. I knew I could trust him. So, I explained everything about Leela and the Lamar apartment building. Hammer agreed we should help Leela, and after breakfast, we went straight downtown. The place was busy for a Sunday. I'd forgotten it was a few days before Christmas, which reminded me that I hadn't done any Christmas shopping yet—something I had to ask Hammer if he wouldn't mind us doing. We drove around for several minutes before finding a parking place, braved the cold weather, and trekked over to Woolworth's—Mom's favorite place to shop. And from the looks of all the people inside, it was everyone else's, too. We braved the crowds, and I bought a few things for Mom, something for Hammer, and several items for Leela, including a blanket. It wasn't big, but I hoped it could help on those cold nights. I was glad Hammer had some money on him since I was a little short. Twenty dollars didn't go as far as I thought. After shopping, I mentioned something to

Hammer that had been on my mind. I wanted to buy a car and get my license. But when I'd said that, I had no idea he was going to stuff me in the driver's seat right then! I was glad he talked me into getting my learner's permit before going to college. The written test went smoothly, so driving couldn't be that difficult. But it was the exact opposite when I climbed behind the wheel. It had been a while since I practiced driving with Mom, and I felt completely out of my element for a few minutes. I clutched the steering wheel with an iron grip and breathed out slowly. I could do this; it would be easy. *Just like riding a bike . . . except, I fell and scraped my knees so many times learning to ride a bike.*

Hammer laughed. "Come on. It's not that difficult! You don't have to be so serious!"

"Ha ha, you're right." I laughed and breathed in deeply, trying to remember how Mom taught me to drive. I turned the key, and the car rumbled to life. He was right, this was easy. I grinned and put my foot to the pedal. The car lurched forward, gunning for the vehicle ahead.

"The brakes!" Hammer screamed. My eyes bugged out as I slammed my foot into the brake pedal, throwing us forward. I groaned as my belly slammed into the steering wheel.

Hammer cast me a look that could only be expressed with words I would not dare say. "Get out of the car."

I rejected his request and demanded he give me another chance. This time I jerked the car forward, then jammed the brakes too hard, and even ran the tire up over the curb pulling out of the parking spot. But after a few minutes and after getting away from the downtown traffic, my nerves calmed down, and I was able to focus a little more. It didn't take long to remember the things Mom had taught me about driving, and everything came flooding back.

We drove around several places. I even practiced parallel parking. It took several attempts to get the car parked correctly, but I beamed with pride when I completed the task. The drive was mostly uneventful for the big trip, and I slowed down as we came into Lamar. I hit the brakes, coming to a stop, but the car rocked slightly and I caught my breath. Did . . . did I just . . .?

"Gerald . . ." Hammer breathed, "I think you should turn off the car."

I went numb. I just rear-ended the car at the stoplight. My hand trembled as I fumbled with the key, unable to turn the car off properly. I couldn't believe I'd just hit someone's car! I misjudged the brakes' sensitivity and grazed the vehicle in front of me at the red light. I was thankful the man was super nice. He understood my situation as he'd recently taught his son how to drive and was quite forgiving. I think it also helped that there was no sign of damage on either car, which also relieved Hammer.

I was surprised he let me continue, but he did, saying it was only a bump in the road to learning. I looked up to Hammer. He was like a father figure. He was kind, caring, and understanding for someone who was only a few years older than me.

I coasted into the apartment building parking lot—the gravel crunching beneath the tires. I took a deep breath. I did it. Hammer assured me I was ready to take my driver's test. He said I was a natural, though I wasn't sold on that yet.

I wanted to go into the building alone, but Hammer wouldn't hear of it. He demanded he go inside, but he would wait on the second floor and let me go alone from there. I agreed. We entered, not sure if we would find her. I carried the small paper sack. It wasn't much—a few cans of beans, a cheap can opener, a half loaf of bread, a pack of lunch meat, and two orange Nehi soda pops. On the note I attached, I instructed her to leave the meat and drinks outside on the window ledge to keep them cold.

I knew Mom would be proud of me for helping someone in need; however, I decided she didn't need to know what I was doing, not yet anyway. I walked over to the bottom step with Hammer on my heels. I glanced upward and placed my foot on the first step. Something came over me. I was nervous and butterflies soared in my stomach. I couldn't explain the feeling. It felt different from the other times when a ghost was near. I thought back to the first time I saw Leela. There was something kind about her eyes.

I crept up the steps past the first and second floor and started up the final flight of steps. I turned and held out my hand to stop Hammer. He understood, and I proceeded alone. "Hello," I called, my voice soft. I crested the top of the stairs and gingerly stepped down the hallway. "It's Gerald. I brought you some food." I stopped, swallowed hard, and poked my head around the last entryway. The smell of ash filled my nostrils, letting me know the fireplace had recently been used. She must be close. Maybe she was hiding from me.

I walked across the floor to the mattress. I stretched my neck, trying to get a glimpse in the closet, but my angle was wrong. I took a step back. I didn't want to frighten her. I needed Leela to trust me. So, I lowered the bag of goods to the floor and stood up. "Merry Christmas, Leela," I said before I turned and walked to the door, pausing once to look back over my shoulder. Then I made my way downstairs.

"Was she there?"

"No," I slumped, "but the fireplace had been recently used."

Hammer nodded like that was a small victory, and I agreed.

Hammer climbed behind the wheel, and I was glad because the sun was setting, and even though I was pretty sure I'd gotten the hang of driving, I'd never driven at night. We didn't say much on the trip home, which gave my mind time as it wandered to Leela a few times. I hope she enjoyed the supplies we had left. The car rolled to a stop, and just like that, we were back at the dorm. Since my roommate Kim was home for Christmas break, Hammer would have a bed to himself.

The next morning, I grabbed my personal belongings and some clothes, stuffing them in my small suitcase. I was finally ready to go and locked the door behind me as I left college for the first time since I'd arrived. I was excited to be going home for a few days to see Mom. I had so much to share with her, and I knew she would be proud of me.

I tossed my bag inside the trunk, and Hammer did the same. We jumped in the car, and Hammer drove us to the bank where Professor Wollensak was waiting for us. We were at the bank longer than I expected. First, the professor showed them the contract that he represented me; otherwise, my mother would have had to do with this me since I was underage. Once the bank teller had reviewed the paperwork, I signed the check, then I filled out a bunch of papers to open my checking and saving accounts.

I thanked them all, and Professor Wollensak, of course. I hopped in the car and flashed my new bank book so Hammer could see. Then I showed him my blank checks. They were only temporary, but they were mine. I always carried a wallet, but today my pocket felt different, maybe because it bulged with cash—I was hoping the hundred dollars would last a while. I smiled with pride; for the first time in my life, I felt independent and confident.

My excitement level grew as we started down the road. I couldn't wait to see Mom. I had friends, excellent grades, and I was going to be a published author. Life was great. Hammer continued to drive, passing through Lamar. I peered in the direction of the apartments. I hoped Leela was enjoying the supplies I left for her.

I had never paid close attention when my mother drove me to college. I never realized we had passed through Lamar. But now, I was more observant of my surroundings. The trip took a little over an hour, but finally, Hammer turned down the street leading to the old neighborhood. I couldn't wait to see Mom's smiling face.

The tires crunched in the gravel driveway as the car thumped to a halt. Hammer sounded the horn a time or two. The front door flew open, almost knocking the wreath off. I was surprised to see that Mom had put up a few Christmas lights this year. The house looked amazing. Mom bounced out with joy and bounded down the stairs. I leaped from the car, not worrying about my bag, and embraced her.

"I'm so happy you're home."

"Me, too."

It felt incredible to hug her again. I didn't realize how much I missed her. She hugged me back with force, and I could tell she was excited to see her little boy. The thought that Mom had never been alone hadn't occurred to me until now, and I wondered why I had never thought of that before. I guess I was too focused on myself. I felt guilty because I hadn't written in over a month and I had only called a few times, because Mom reminded me that collect calls were expensive. As much as I wanted to call, I couldn't burden her with an expensive phone bill. Plus, I enjoyed the letters she wrote me, but now, I felt selfish. I'll have to make sure I write to her more often next semester. Maybe I'll even get special stationery that I will use just for her.

She ushered Hammer and me inside the house where Hammer placed my bag in the hallway. Mom fixed dinner for us, just like old times, and we reminisced over the past few months.

I lay in my bed for the first time in months. I yawned and stretched, and my eyelids felt so heavy. My mind, however, had other plans. I frowned when I thought back to our dinner conversation, and how Mom didn't share the same feelings about publishing my stories. I think she was worried for me heading out into this big cruel world all by myself. She'd always been my protector. Perhaps it was the subject I chose to write about. Who knows? I didn't want to dwell on it. I only wanted to sleep.

I tossed and turned, trying to sleep. Oddly enough, it wasn't Mom I thought of. It was Leela. The mystery girl in the apartment building weighed heavily on my mind. That was the last thing I remembered when I woke in the morning.

I didn't feel right about giving Mom money for Christmas—it wasn't personal. So, I decided to buy her a few gifts. I wanted this to be a Christmas she would remember. I convinced Hammer to give me a lift to town to do some last-minute shopping.

* * *

Christmas morning I bounced out of bed and leaped down the stairs as I had when I was younger. I caught a whiff of the turkey as Mom worked away in the kitchen. I peered into the living room and much to my surprise, there were more presents than I had expected.

"Gerald, is that you?"

"Who else would it be, Mom?"

"I invited Deloris, Rob, and Bates over." She turned as I entered the kitchen. "Would you like some pancakes and syrup?"

"Yes, ma'am." Mom made the best homemade pancakes, and my stomach growled in anticipation. I pulled out the chair and lowered myself in and began to eat when she sat a tall stack in front of me.

"Slow down, the presents will wait." She shot me a sidelong smile. "When you're done eating, go get yourself ready before our guests arrive."

"Sure thing." I finished my breakfast, walked over, wrapped my arms around my mom, and held her tight. I didn't realize how much I missed her. I was going to do a better job of keeping in touch during the second half of the school year.

The shower refreshed me—another reminder of how good it was to be home. I slipped on a nice clean shirt and jeans, then started down the stairs. No sooner than I rounded the corner, I found myself in a headlock.

"Bates, this is Christmas!" his mother shouted.

"Sorry, Mom." He rubbed my head one last time and released his grip.

"Hello, Mr. and Mrs. Bergen."

"Good morning, Gerald, and Merry Christmas," Hammer's father added.

"Merry Christmas, everyone." I strolled over and gave them each a hug.

Mom ushered everyone to the living room. I took my spot next to the tree with Hammer on the opposite side next to a large box. It was like we were kids all over again.

I was the youngest, so naturally, I got to open presents first. I grabbed the gift from Hammer and tore the wrapping off. I gasped when I saw a nice set of notebooks and a pen set. "Dude, these are awesome! Thank you." I could use these to write my next novel. I continued to open the next gift—a nice pair of jeans and two pairs of dress slacks from Mom, along with three nice dress shirts. I was going to look sharp in class now. She also bought me a new set of encyclopedias for when I came home during the summer. I couldn't help but get choked up with her generosity.

Hammer was next, and he ripped open the package from me. He was stunned that I bought him a nice set of Craftsmen screwdrivers. I wanted him to be the best mechanic in town. His eyes squinted, and his face twitched. I knew I had touched a nerve, and I returned his smile. He was floored as he pulled the wrapping off to reveal a large metal toolbox from his parents. It was nice to see the big guy let loose and shed some tears.

Finally, it was Mom's turn. I bounced on my knees as she opened the first gift and held up a plush, full-length bathrobe. "Oh, Gerald, you shouldn't have," she choked out.

"I love you, Mom."

"There's another gift from Gerald." She looked at me and frowned. "You didn't need to get me two gifts." I smiled back and nudged the present closer to her.

She plucked the wrapping off, savoring every second, to reveal a new colored Polaroid camera and two packs of film. She blushed and tears ran down her face. She dropped to her knees and gave me a giant hug.

"You're the best mom ever," I whispered in her ear.

* * *

This had turned out to be the best Christmas ever, and with the pictures we took, the memories would last forever. The only downside was it was time to go back to college. After another home-cooked breakfast, I carried my bag to the car and tossed it in the trunk. I turned and smothered Mom with a hug. "I had a wonderful Christmas," I whispered as a tear tracked down my cheek. "I love you, Mom. Thank you for everything you do for me."

"I love you too, Gerald." The air oozed from my lungs as she clamped her arms around me. "Now hurry along. You don't want to keep Bates waiting." She released me and ran back to the porch in her plush new robe. I climbed in the front seat and slammed the door as I discreetly tried to wipe my watering eyes. I knew this wasn't going to be easy, but I didn't think it would be this hard leaving home again. The engine roared, and we backed out of the driveway. I looked back once to wave, but the door had already closed.

CHAPTER EIGHTEEN

We had several days before classes would resume, and I was thrilled that Hammer decided to stick around a little longer. My roommate Kim, who had even mentioned that Hammer's visits needed to stop, was not so excited. I assured him they would, thinking Hammer could stay in Gannon's room or even at Fang's.

We made another trip to the apartment building to drop off more supplies for Leela. The food I had left before had vanished, though I was surprised that I didn't see any empty cans or wrappers. I guess Leela was tidy, something I could relate to. The fact that the food was gone was a good sign. It told me someone or something was eating it.

I still hadn't seen any sign of Leela since the ghost hunt, and I was beginning to get worried. Had something happened to her? Had she moved on? If so, then who was eating the food? I looked over my shoulder at Hammer. I was thankful to him for bringing me here, but maybe she only trusted me. We left the food and headed back to the campus.

I needed to pass my driver's test and buy a car; that would solve my problems. I mentioned that to Hammer, so we stopped at a few used car lots on the way home. One car had caught my eye—a 1960 mint-green Corvair Monza Coupe. It was a sleek little car and one of the first to have the engine mounted in the rear. Hammer said it was the car of the future.

After a grueling afternoon of car shopping, we returned to the dorm. As the thoughts ran around my head and I contemplated how to meet Leela, someone banged on my door. I sprang to my feet, rushed to the door, and flung it open.

"Long time no see!"

"Gannon!" I cried, throwing myself at him.

He returned my hug before taking a step back. "How was your Christmas?"

"Ah, you know." I smiled. "I got some new clothes."

"Me, too." He laughed.

"How are you doing?" Hammer threw a giant-sized bear hug on Gannon.

"Struggling to breathe," Gannon squeaked, and we laughed as Hammer set Gannon down.

"Oh man, you are not going to believe this." I grabbed the publishing contract from my desk and tossed it to Gannon.

His eyes bulged as he thumbed through the pages. "That's awesome." He shook his head in disbelief. "Now, you can pay me back for all those lunches I treated you to."

"I have every intention," I said as I handed Gannon a twenty-dollar bill.

He shoved the money back into my hand. "Man, I was only kidding!"

"Please." I extended my hand, holding the bill out to him.

"Keep your money, but I will let you buy my dinner,"

I nodded and pocketed the bill. "Deal." I grabbed my jacket, and the three of us headed out. We strolled down the sidewalk. I shared that it was great seeing my mother and how much I missed her. Gannon was thrilled that I decided to spend some time away from school.

I was taken back when Gannon mentioned his sister was doing great in high school. "I didn't know you had a sister."

"Maybe he doesn't want you hitting on his sister." Hammer jabbed me in the arm with a chuckle.

"I wouldn't do that," I said, and they almost fell over in laughter. I snickered back; I could tell they didn't believe me.

We decided to stop at the Eagles Nest for dinner. Why spend our money when we can eat for free at the cafeteria? As we entered, I spotted Dee, Gabe, Angel, and Sam sitting at a table by themselves. This was turning out to be a grand day. The gang was back together, and everyone was excited to see us.

I noticed lots of familiar faces in the dining hall. I wasn't surprised to see Desmond and Sandy sitting together at a private table tucked away in the corner. I guess they were still a thing. I almost didn't recognize Sandy. Gone were the ponytails, and her straight blonde hair flowed past her shoulders. It was a good look for her, and I was happy for both of them, though it made me feel kind of lonely. Was I that different from everyone else? Was I incapable of making a girl happy?

Why haven't I ever heard Gannon complain about not having a girl in his life? Was having a girl that important to me? I'll visit that later. I turned my attention back to the others. We carried on our conversation for hours. I mostly listened, chiming in when necessary. It seemed everyone had a terrific time over the holiday break as they shared stories of hanging out with their family and some friends who came back into town, what they had for Christmas dinner, and of course, what they got for Christmas.

Gabe agreed to take me for my driver's test. That worked in my favor because Hammer had to return home for work Monday morning. I was nervous but thrilled at the same time. All I had to do was pass, and I would be that much closer to freedom.

The first week back to class was like any other, with tons of homework and very little time to do anything but study. I only added one new class this semester—creative writing with Professor Wollensak, who was delighted to see me sitting in the front row.

I finally had some free time on Wednesday afternoon. Gabe met me outside near the dorms, leaning against his beat-up wagon. "Hey, man! Thanks for taking me!"

"No problem," he said, slapping me on the back. "Get inside; you've got yourself a test to pass!"

The drive was a short one, and soon we arrived at a small hovel of a building that looked something like a shed. From my view, the road course looked small but sloped downward. I took a few quick breaths, going through the steps in my mind. "Are you ready?" the instructor asked me.

"Ready," I responded. I would pass this test with sheer determination, if nothing else! And so, I turned the key. Gabe's wagon was larger than Hammer's sedan, and that made things more challenging. But by the skin of my teeth, I passed! Thank goodness Hammer let me practice several times over Christmas break. I held my head high and tucked my new driver's license into my wallet.

With the weekend approaching, I was hoping to pick up my new car. It was a used car, but new to me. Gabe dropped me off first thing Saturday morning, with Gannon at my side. I was in luck. The 1960 mint-green Corvair Monza Coupe was available. There was something about that car that I loved. We sat down and worked out the terms and signed all the papers. I was a car owner! Though now I have to pay sixty-eight dollars a month for the next three years. But with my book royalties, I felt confident I would be able to make the payments with ease.

I must have looked like an idiot while I waited for the salesman to finish up the paperwork. I couldn't stop smiling, but when the salesman handed me the keys, I almost cried. I was so ecstatic, I wanted to scream and dance around, but since Gannon was with me, I was able to keep it together.

The talk on campus was about a new restaurant that opened—McDonald's. So, of course, that was the first place I decided to drive to. I wrapped my hands around the steering wheel and squeezed a few times.

"Are you going to play with the wheel or drive?"

"Sorry." My smile was still ear to ear. I turned the key and listened to the engine purr, and then I put the car into motion. We drove a few blocks, and there it was. Giant golden arches leaping over the roof, stretching from front to back on each side of the building. The sign out front was a giant M, with a large red sign in the middle that read 'wonderful hamburgers.' It was the first fast-food restaurant to come to our neck of the woods, and lunch was on me that day. Fifteen-cent-burgers and twelve-cents for fries was a steal. Now, this was a place I could afford to dine more often.

Later that day, Gannon and I made our way to Fang's. Everyone was there except for Hammer. *I missed the big lug.* They took turns climbing in and out of the Corvair. Fang, Gabe, and Sam were fascinated with the rear engine and the front storage compartment located under the hood. I took each of them for a ride around the block. With me owning a car, we could now add new members to the team and carry more equipment! I beamed with pride and was proud of my contribution to the team.

As the gang fawned over my new car, I felt extra generous, so I sprang for pizza from the Snack Shack. As soon as the sun set, we packed up the cars and headed west to Mill Hall. There was only room for two in my car, so of course, I chose Gannon as my copilot. But I didn't know how to get to the axe factory, so I stayed close behind Gabe.

The evening air was crisp, not too hot and not too cold—the perfect night for a ghost hunt. Rumor had it, there were several murders at the factory, and a few folks had gone missing with no explanation as to what had happened.

Darkness made for low vision, and as this was my first time driving at night, it posed some new challenges. I squinted a few times, staring at the bright red lights on the back of Gabe's car. I was thankful he didn't drive fast. Moments later, we passed through Mill Hall. This was my first time seeing this place. It was a small town of five or six hundred people nestled along the banks of fishing creek. Downtown was small, with a school located at one end and a church at the other. Burrowed in the middle, I saw a family restaurant, a grocery store, a bank, a barbershop, and a bar. The rest of downtown was made up of small houses or apartment buildings.

The streetlights faded behind us, and mountains closed in on both sides as we passed through the valley. The road twisted and turned, following the contour of the mountain. High rocks beamed upward on one side, with the creek nestled below on the other.

We drove a little farther until we came to a strange sign. Welcome to Lizardville. *How weird was that for a town name?* Gabe slowed, and I observed his turn signal. We cascaded down a small incline into an open field, and I pulled my car alongside Gabe's.

I turned the engine off and gazed out the window. Jerking the handle of the car door, I stepped into the crisp night air. Stars twinkled in and out, dodging behind the clouds. My eyes adjusted to the light. Fireflies dotted the landscape, and the distant roar of water cascading over the falls echoed through the air. It was a picturesque backdrop for a ghost hunt.

We grabbed our gear as Fang barked out orders. I focused my attention on the factory and quickly fell in step behind the others. "Stay close," someone hollered. I quickened my pace with Gannon on my heels, dirt crunching beneath our boots.

Clouds shifted and the moon brightened. I had a clear view of the factory. It appeared smaller than I had imagined. To my left, I could see the dam stretching out over the water—a slender two-story building located in the middle of the concrete structure. I wondered if we would venture up the stairs to the overlook room.

We huddled near the entrance. "Gather round," Fang instructed, and we pulled into a tight half-circle. "This is the main factory. Legend has it, a few workers died here. Some by accident, others took their own lives. One man was said to have gone missing and was never found."

Fang pointed to a small house on the other side of the road. I couldn't help but notice all the fireflies dancing in the night sky. "That was the owner's house. They say his wife died in the house by a violent attack from an employee." Fang changed directions, pointing toward the dam. "Over here, it's said that careless workers drowned in the swirling waters. No one knows how many ghosts reside here. So, stay alert. Oh, and remember one thing, tonight we walk with the dead. Any questions?" I had a few but kept my mouth shut after Fang's creepy pep talk.

"What are the teams?" Donnie asked.

"I almost forgot. Gabe, Dee, Sam, and Angel," Fang pointed to each of them as he called their names, "take the dam and the overlook tower. Gannon, Gerald, Donnie, and I will start in the factory." Fang smiled.

"What channel?" Sam asked, slightly waving the walkie-talkie back and forth.

"Nine."

Donnie turned the knob and fell in step behind Fang as we made our way inside the factory. My heart raced. I don't care how many times I do this, I get a rush that can't be described.

I looked over my shoulder to Gannon and noticed the broad grin on his face, one that matched mine.

I stepped over the threshold to the sound of crunching glass beneath my shoes. My flashlight darted back and forth, streaming beams of light on the concrete. The floor was covered with debris, overgrown weeds, and brush, and wooden workbenches lined the walls. For the most part, the large hall was empty. I followed Fang to the middle of the floor. We cleared a small circle and set up our folding stools. I took my seat, our backs facing each other to give each of us a great view should something appear. One by one, we flicked off the flashlights. Gannon turned on the cassette recorder, I readied my camera, and the wait began.

The screech of a hoot owl cawed in the distance. Most likely, it killed its prey and was now enjoying the meal. A whispering breeze rolled through the broken windows, sending chills down my spine. I fumbled around with the zipper on my jacket but realized it was already tight around my neck. The waiting was the worst part of ghost hunting, mainly the hours of silence. The first hours passed without incident. The clouds gave way to the moon, sending a beam of light racing over the floor.

I paused to look around and listened carefully. It was quiet, not even the sound of a chirping cricket. This was it, the moment of truth. I felt a sensation in my stomach. I knew for sure something was about to happen. I sat straight on the edge of my stool. I heard a squeak, then another. I noticed my fingers were tingling. I glanced at my hand and saw it balled into a fist. I bit my lip and stretched my fingers to let them relax when I heard the noise again.

Something nudged my ankle, and my eyes raced downward. Fang clicked the light on, and I shot to my feet like I was fired from a cannon. "It's a rat. I hate rats." I danced about and continued to scream, and I scared the poor fellow away. I trembled for a minute as the others enjoyed a good laugh at my expense.

Gannon nudged my shoulder. "Get a grip, man."

"How would you feel if a rat attacked you?"

"You weren't attacked." Fang chuckled.

"If it helps, I'm not getting any vibes." I snorted. "Maybe we should move to another location?"

Donnie squeezed his finger on the trigger of the walkie-talkie. "Sam, do you copy?"

"We copy."

"See anything?"

"Negative."

"Meet us outside in five."

"Copy that."

We stood, and Fang laid a hand on my shoulder. "We should check out the owner's house."

I nodded.

"If you feel up to it."

"I'm good." I nodded again, trying to convince myself and the others I was okay with checking out the house. I bent over and grabbed my stool, and once again, I fell in step behind the boys. I walked through the doorway to the shock of the frigid cold air. I was stunned at how fast the temperature had dropped. But this was Pennsylvania in January, and things could change in a minute.

I heard voices before I noticed Gabe and Dee's silhouettes holding hands as they came into view. Angel and Sam were a step behind. "Are we packing it in?" Sam asked.

"We could check out the house across the street before we leave." Fang pointed. Without saying another word, Fang and Donnie started moving in that direction.

A shiver ran up my spine. "Stay away," someone whispered. I paused before being shoved in the back.

"What'd you stop for?" Gannon asked.

"I heard something."

Fang and Donnie stopped dead in their tracks and turned to face me. "What did you hear?" Curiosity riddled Donnie's voice.

A man's voice whispered in my ear again, "Stay away."

"Did you hear that?" My eyes darted back and forth. "Is it just me? Am I the only one hearing him?"

Gannon pressed his hand to my shoulder. "I guess so. What did you hear?"

"This must sound crazy, but he told me to stay away."

"That's it?" Fang paced in a circle. "That makes no sense. We've been here for hours, so why now?" I could tell Fang was frustrated. "We're missing something. Come on, guys, think," Fang barked.

"That's what I heard. The voice was clear and precise." I wracked my brain, trying to understand the message.

"I don't get it," Gannon added.

We stood in a circle staring at each other before Fang chimed in, "Let's check out the house, and then we'll call it a night." Fang motioned with his hand and started walking across the field.

"Stop!" the voice called out.

I froze. "He said, stop. He's trying to tell us something, but what?"

We looked at each other for a few moments. "This is ridiculous. Let's go," Gabe demanded.

I glanced at the house across the street, keeping in step with the others. I had a bad feeling about this. It was apparent the ghost wanted us to stay away. What magic lay behind those doors? We would soon find out.

Fang and Donnie stopped next to the cars. Out of the corner of my eye, I noticed a set of bright lights making their way toward us. We weren't alone. Someone or something was coming.

"Duck," Fang blurted out.

We crouched behind the cars and sat motionless as we waited with anticipation. The lights slowed almost to a stop. I could tell it was a car, but was it the police? I didn't think we had broken any rules. We were just a group of college kids gathered in a small field overlooking the dam.

Great minds think alike; Gannon must have read my mind. "We came here to listen to the water flow over the dam. It's peaceful and relaxing," Gannon whispered. Everyone nodded in agreement. That was a good story. Much to our surprise, the car turned to the right and pulled into the driveway across the street. Brake lights glared, and the dome light flared as the doors opened.

A tall man stepped out of the driver's door, and a woman appeared on the passenger's side. Not one, or two, but three children hustled out of the rear seat before running toward the porch. We watched in amazement as the man and woman closed the doors behind them, making their way to the front door. The man fumbled with his keys, and finally, the front door swung open and the lights clicked on.

The woman and children vanished behind the door, but the man remained on the porch. I watched as he fumbled with his pocket and slowly raised his hand. A small flame ignited when he lit a cigarette.

"I'll be damned. Someone lives there," Donnie murmured.

"I think the voice was protecting us from going to the house."

"That's crazy, Gerald," Fang's voice erupted, louder than he meant to.

The man stepped off the porch and made his way toward his car and opened the trunk. A large beam of light darted around the yard, then across the road in our direction. "Is someone there?" he shouted. "I heard you; now show yourself!"

"Let's get out of here," Angel whispered.

Car doors flew open. The scramble was on—bodies flying around and climbing over each other into the station wagon. "Gerald," Gannon pulled on my sleeve, "open the doors," he said with a touch of panic in his voice.

Then it hit me like a slap in the face. I was driving. Desperately, I shoved my hand into my pocket, trying to free my keys. They sprang out, landing in the tall grass. Furiously, I tried to find them.

"Hey, what are you kids doing over there?" the man yelled, sounding angry.

"Gerald, open the door."

My fingers darted around in an endless battle to find the keys. Dirt, twigs, grass, weeds, nothing useful. The roar of an engine rang through the night as Gabe fired up his wagon. His brake lights illuminated the ground. The glare was enough for me to spot something shiny. I wrapped my hands around the keys and sighed in relief.

"Gerald!" Gannon barked again.

I straightened up and slid the key into the door slot with ease and turned. The door sprung open, and I fell into the driver's seat and immediately stretched my arm to lift the door lock on the passenger door. The door flung open, and Gannon crawled inside. I bobbled the keys, trying to put them in the ignition, but only wasted a few seconds before I found the hole and heard the purr of the engine. I jammed the handle on the steering column down into the drive position and slammed the gas pedal to the floor.

My rear tires spun on the damp grass, leaving a trail of rock and debris behind. I turned the steering wheel as fast as I could, and in a flash, we were charging toward the exit. I thought I heard him shout something as we faded out of sight.

"Man, was that cool or what?"

"If you hadn't dropped the keys, maybe."

"Man, I was as cool as a cucumber."

"Don't kid yourself! You were Mr. Panic."

"Oh, come on. You know I was calm and cool." I didn't care what Gannon said. In my mind, I was Captain Cool. After the initial rush, we laughed most of the way to Fang's. We were stunned that a family lived in the house, and we could still feel the thrill of our narrow escape.

CHAPTER NINETEEN

Last night had been fun but also an uneventful waste of time. Unless, of course, you consider the rat that nearly ate my leg off or the older coot who chased us down the highway. That being said, I know I heard a voice. But was that my subconscious talking to me? Or was it a ghost? I'm not a hundred percent sure. So, obviously, we scratched the dam off our list of haunted locations.

* * *

The week passed quickly. Professor Wollensak stood and dismissed the class and wished all of us a good weekend, then reminded everyone, on our way out of the door, to read chapters eleven through fourteen. The good news was I had already read those chapters earlier in the week. I couldn't help but be excited as I walked back to Decan Hall. I remembered Hammer saying he was coming into town today. I think he's hooked on ghost hunting as much as I am.

I quickened my pace with excitement, rounded the final street corner, glanced toward the student parking lot, and noticed Hammer's car parked next to mine. I found myself running the last hundred yards.

I threw the door open and bounced up the steps and down the hallway to Gannon's room, rapped my knuckles on the door before I pushed the door inward, and was picked up in a flash with a big bear hug. "Good to see you, little buddy." Hammer smiled down at me as he set me back on the floor.

"It's about time," Gannon said, his voice laced with sarcasm.

"Sorry, the professor talked longer than expected," I replied.

"Yea, yea, don't blame others because you're late—" Gannon stopped mid-sentence.

"I wasn't, okay, maybe a little." I chuckled and pushed my glasses back up on my nose.

"Who's hungry?" Hammer belted out.

That was all I needed to hear. I ran to my room, dropped off my books, slipped on my black T-shirt and a fresh pair of jeans, grabbed my coat, and made my way downstairs to hook up with Hammer and Gannon. We strolled across the parking lot and crawled into Hammer's car because it had more room than mine. Hammer wanted pizza, and we knew exactly where to go, the Snack Shack. Instead of calling our order in, we stopped unannounced. The place had become a favorite of ours. I dashed to the counter and ordered three large pepperoni and ham pizzas, enough bottled Pepsi for everyone, and sprung for two bags of Hanover pretzels.

Hammer ran to the Grand Slam pinball machine and dropped in a quarter for three plays. I started to sit on the long wooden bench that skirted the front window but decided to watch Hammer play. He pulled back the firing pin and released, sending the silver ball out into the playing field. The metal ball bounced around the bases. I was never big on playing the games, but the Snack Shack had a brand-new shiny machine with fancy lights flickering in and out. It looked groovy and was named the Beatniks—I think they were a rock-and-roll band, but I wasn't much into music either, as I spent most of my time with my head in a book. But this was a new day, and I was feeling adventurous, so Gannon and I decided to play Beatniks. It was a two-player game. I grabbed a quarter from my pocket and slid it in the slot, then watched as the machine came to life. "I'll go first," I said confidently, pulling back the plunger and blasting the ball upward into the play zone. I watched it bounce back and forth, and I hit the ball a few times with the paddle when it dropped in my direction. My turn didn't last long as the metal ball flashed past the paddle and plunged out of sight.

Gannon stepped up to the machine and let the ball fly. I watched as the steel ball ricocheted off one guitar bumper to another, and then to the drum set. The metal ball deflected and rebounded over and over again. Gannon was pretty good with pinball. I watched the digit counter spin as his score surpassed mine. I did my best to top his score on my next turn, but he'd built such a lead I was unable to catch up. We played a few more games while we waited, and my score improved every time. I think with a little practice, I could get pretty good at pinball. I stepped back and watched Gannon and Hammer play. These were the type of memories I would cherish forever.

"Da pickle man," the dude snickered as he hollered my name from behind the counter. *If I could only change my last name,* I chuckled inside, giving the man no satisfaction because, let's face it, now I didn't have to leave a tip. I threw a few bills on the counter and waited for my change. I scooped up the boxes while Gannon grabbed the sodas and pretzels, and we dashed out the door.

The group was all here, and they were excited that we brought dinner—it was the least I could do for my friends. We dug in, devouring each slice until Angel started gagging.

"Are you alright?" Dee asked as she patted and rubbed Angel's back.

"I'm fine." Angel continued to cough. "It went down the wrong throat," she spat out and tried to regain herself.

"What? You have two throats?" I asked.

The room erupted with laughter.

"Of course not. It went down the wrong pipe," she corrected herself.

"You had us a little worried there." Sam laughed.

"Shut up." She poked Sam and Donnie and gave Fang the evil eye.

I leaned back and decided it was best if I kept my mouth shut.

We demolished the pizzas quicker than any group should. Then we relaxed on the couch, but not for long.

"Tonight's hunt is going to be a little different." Fang dove right into things and paused to look around the room. "The owner says his apartment building is haunted. The only difference is that people live there." Mouths hung open, mine included. My mind raced; how would this work with people walking around?

"How are we gonna—" Fang raised a hand, cutting Donnie off mid-sentence.

"Please hold your questions." He lowered his hand. "The owner told me there had been sightings in the basement, the laundry room, and room 207. Some of the tenants say they've seen things move in the hallways, and even reported strange noises coming from the laundry room after it's closed for the night." Everyone appeared as puzzled as me. Fang raised his hands like he was pushing something back, and we all fell silent.

"Here's my plan. We go in and set up shop in the basement. We will take turns visiting the laundry room and room 207. We document and take plenty of photos and report anything suspicious. I say we observe and see what we can find out, and then we can take the info and make a plan to present to the owner." He nodded to us all. "Oh, did I mention he's paying us fifty dollars? That's right, we have our first paying job!"

"That's five dollars each," Donnie mentioned.

"Actually, it's five dollars and fifty-five cents each. When you factor in how many hours we will be on location and divide five-fifty-five, we won't even make minimum wage." I noticed everyone was gawking at me. "What?" Hammer shook his head at me, so I pinched my fingers together and zipped my mouth shut.

"Well, let's see how things turn out before we go spending the money." Fang's response pulled the attention away from me. I nodded, keeping my thoughts to myself. We were to meet at nine o'clock, which was late for starting a ghost hunt, but that was what the owner wanted.

When the time came, we loaded the cars and made our way to Mill Hall. We arrived a few minutes early and pulled around the back of the building, as the owner requested. The building wasn't large, three floors above ground, with the basement making it four floors. We sat in the station wagon and waited. Ten, fifteen minutes passed before a pickup truck pulled alongside our car. A tall, gangly man wearing a baseball cap stepped out as he wrapped himself in his coat. Fang greeted him and pointed to the rest of us. He seemed excited that we'd showed up. I was not sure what he expected from us—it wasn't like we were going to be able to remove the ghost from the building, at least not on this visit. I had instructions in my upcoming novel on how to cross a spirit over, but I'd only tried it once and wasn't even sure it had worked. But I hadn't seen Victoria since that night, so it was an unproven theory.

The man handed Fang an envelope and a ring of keys. I assumed the envelope contained the money Fang had mentioned. The gentleman shook Fang's hand and wished us luck before he returned to his truck. I got the impression he was frightened of ghosts with how quickly he exited the parking lot.

The doors flung open, and I followed Hammer and Gannon to the rear of the car and picked up a box. We then stepped in line behind the others as we moved to the basement door. The keys jingled in Fang's hands as he fumbled to open the door. Moments later, the door sprang free, and we marched forward. I looked over Gannon's shoulder and found the room was dark. A beam of light cast over the stairs when Fang turned on his flashlight, and one by one, we descended into the basement.

The place looked like any other basement, with boxes piled up in one corner and old furniture scattered here and there, covered with dusty sheets. It was damp and had a musty smell that irritated my nose. I detected the faint smell of urine and then noticed a cat litter box in the corner. I didn't see any cats, but that didn't mean they weren't present—they're masters at hiding. A large workbench ran along the far wall, tools scattered along its surface. The urge to explore hit me like a tidal wave. I felt the need to unpack the boxes to see what treasures lurked inside. I imagined the boxes held items left behind from prior tenants. But I was brought back to why we were here when Fang started barking out orders.

We huddled in a large circle, while Donnie, Sam, and Gabe set up the folding chairs and unpacked our tools. I grabbed my new Polaroid camera and handed Hammer my cassette recorder. I kept looking over my shoulder at the pile of boxes. Was there something inside I needed to see?

"Gerald," Fang barked.

My head spun around. "Yes."

"Getting any vibes?"

"No, not yet." I wasn't feeling anything. It was just a typical basement. Maybe I'd get that strange sensation when we went upstairs.

"We'll take turns walking the hallways, so we don't raise suspicions."

"Why doesn't he want the tenants to know we're here?" *I was always the curious one*.

"He doesn't want them to think the place is haunted because they might leave or ask for reduced rent." Fang swayed back and forth. "Does that answer your question?"

"Sure does."

"Okay then, Gerald, Hammer, and I will go to room 207 and see what's inside and report back," Fang said as he turned the knob on his walkie-talkie. "Channel nine everyone." I watched the others do the same.

Fang motioned with his head, and I followed with Hammer on my heels. I noticed a dumbwaiter next to the bottom of the stairs. My thoughts raced to the Lamar Apartments. That must be how Leela was getting around. I hadn't noticed one in the wall, but I hadn't been looking for one, either. It was a small elevator about the size of a large ice chest used for moving food, bed linens, and cleaning supplies between floors. If she ducked inside and closed the door, she could lower herself to a different floor or even go in-between floors to hide. I had to give her credit; she was one smart cookie. "Are you coming?" Fang yelled from the top of the stairwell.

Hammer nudged me in the back. "You okay, Gerald?"

"Sure, I noticed the dumbwaiter, and it got me thinking, that's all." I hurried up the stairs and caught up to Fang. He nudged the door open a little and looked to make sure the coast was clear before proceeding into the corridor. Tiptoeing down the passage, I could feel Hammer breathing down my neck. I heard the sound of a television playing as we passed the first door. The faint sound of music echoed under the door a little farther down the hallway. We passed the elevator and headed for the stairs.

Fang pushed the door open and we ducked inside. We marched upward to the second-floor landing, where Fang paused to check and see if our path was clear. We continued forward and down the hallway and stopped in front of a plain white door with black numbers 207 painted on it. Fang turned the keys over and over in his hands, trying several keys before he found the one that clicked the lock open. The door swung inward, and we ducked inside without being seen.

Fang switched on the lights, and we found the place was move-in ready. The room had a sofa, a chair, and a coffee table pushed against the wall, with a small table on the opposite side of the room that would have probably held a TV set. We trekked across the room and glanced in the kitchen. A stove, refrigerator, and a table with four chairs filled the room. Nothing unusual here. At the end was a small bathroom, and I felt the urge to use it but resisted. We backtracked out of the kitchen into the living room and then to the other door. Behind that door was a lovely-sized bedroom—a good mattress set, a wooden chest of drawers, and even a matching dresser.

Fang went back into the living room, flicked the lights off, and plopped down on the couch. I took the recliner while Hammer sat next to Fang. "Now what?" Hammer asked.

I already knew the answer to that question. *We wait!*

I grazed my hand along the side of the cushioned chair and found a small wooden handle and pulled back until the chair folded out. Oh, this baby was comfortable. We sat in silence and listened, and I may have closed my eyes for a bit.

We heard voices coming from the hallway from time to time, but I wasn't picking up any feelings or vibes from the apartment. Nothing at all; this place didn't feel haunted. We must have been in the room for over an hour when the radio sprang to life, and Gabe's voice echoed, "Any luck, guys?"

"All's quiet," Fang responded.

"Same here." I detected a hint of disappointment in his voice.

We sat, waited, then finally made our way back to the basement. Sam and Angel took the next shift sitting in the room while the rest of us sat quietly on the fold-out camping stools in the basement. We took turns strolling through the hallways about every thirty minutes.

The midnight hour approached, and we knew if something were going to happen, it would be soon. My heart raced a little with hopes of seeing another ghost. My legs began to twitch. I was growing restless and wished I would have brought a book. Another hour had come and gone. Maybe the place wasn't haunted. I didn't sense anything, and usually, I'm pretty good at reading my feelings.

It was after two in the morning before Fang decided to call the night. We met the others downstairs in the basement and packed up. Then Gannon suggested we go back to the Lamar apartment building tomorrow night.

"Technically, Gannon, it's not tomorrow night since we're already in the morning." I paused. "It would be tonight," I said, though my tone was sharper than I meant. I guess I panicked. I wasn't ready to have the group discover Leela, not yet anyway. Not to mention it wouldn't be nice to bring the gang along without warning her first. "How about we go back to the Blue Owl Inn?" I threw out the suggestion with wide eyes and gazed at the others in the room.

"We've been there twice, and the last time was kind of scary, if you ask me," Gannon fired back.

“I agree with Gannon. I enjoy ghost hunting, and Lily seemed nice in a way, but the old man wanted to kill us. I don’t think it’s worth risking our lives,” Fang added.

“Let’s vote on it?” Donnie threw out. “Raise your hand for the Lamar apartments.”

I looked around the room and everyone had raised their hand for Lamar, excluding Hammer and me, of course. I sank but had no choice but to go along with what everyone else wanted. I don’t know why I felt the need to protect Leela, especially since I’d only met her a few times. Why haven’t I told the group about her? It was a feeling I couldn’t explain, not yet anyway. Could it be that I liked her?

“Well, that settles it. Tomorrow, I mean . . . tonight, my place at seven p.m.” Fang swayed.

I wanted to stomp around the room in protest but knew better. I was past those days of throwing a tantrum. My heart sank. I had no way of warning Leela that we were coming!

CHAPTER TWENTY

I woke after a good night's sleep and glanced around the room. Hammer was huddled on the floor next to my bed. My roommate wasn't thrilled that Hammer had slept over, but I'd also had to endure his friends a time or two. I mentioned to Kim that this would be the last time as we were making other arrangements.

Panic set in as I thought about tonight's ghost hunt. How could I warn Leela? Why was I even protecting her? Could I sneak out without waking Hammer? He looked tired, and I wouldn't be gone long. I could drive to Lamar and let Leela know we were coming. I quietly placed a foot on the floor, and then the other; then I tiptoed across the room and creaked opened the door.

"Hey, don't be too long. I need to go." Hammer stirred under his blanket.

Crap! My plan was foiled. "Sure, I'll be quick." I stepped outside and walked down the hall to the bathroom. *I was not too fond of the fact that I had no way to warn Leela.* I smiled as another idea popped into my head. I could suggest we take two cars. Then I could have Hammer beep the horn when we arrived! *That might work.* It would allow her enough time to realize someone was there. As I finished, Hammer banged on the stall door.

"Hurry open before I go on the floor." He laughed and went into the stall next to mine.

I slung the door open and let it slam behind me. I needed a shower. I went back to my room, gathered my things, and hollered through the door where I was heading. Hammer acknowledged and said he would be there shortly.

I felt refreshed after my shower, and now my tummy was growling. I returned to the room, tossed my clothes into the hamper, stretched with a yawn, and then paused.

The light was streaming through the window. I squinted. *What time is it?* I glanced at the clock on the wall and noticed it was one p.m. I stood shocked that we had slept all morning and into the afternoon. I tugged my pants on, tied my shoes, and slid my black shirt over my head before tossing my coat over my shoulder. I passed Hammer in the hallway and told him I was heading to wake Gannon. I knocked on Gannon's door and watched as he dashed around, getting ready, then headed back to my room to grab Hammer.

It didn't take much to convince Hammer to drive and nudge the horn when we arrived. He didn't understand why I didn't tell the group about Leela, and it was something I was struggling with, too.

It was a little after two before we made it to the car. We decided to head straight to Fang's to see if he wanted to join us for a hoagie. We knocked on the door and waited forever. Fang had been listening to recordings from our last few ghost hunts and compared them to the notes in his logbook. That explained why he didn't answer right away. While he was shocked to see the three of us this early in the day, he was thrilled to join us for lunch.

We piled into the car and darted over to the Snack Shack. Their hoagies tasted marvelous. I sank my teeth in, and the soft bread melted in my mouth. We gathered around the pinball machines—they were addictive—and played for what seemed like hours. Gannon was the first to notice it was a little after six, reminding us we needed to meet the others around seven.

We enjoyed one final game before venturing back to the apartment. I think we were all surprised when we pulled up and noticed Gabe, Dee, Sam, Angel, and Donnie were already waiting.

"Where you been?" Gabe demanded. "It's freaking cold out here."

"We were hanging out at the Snack Shack," Fang countered, starting up the stairs as the rest of us fell in step behind him. It wasn't long before we had all our gear packed and the cars loaded. Darkness set in, and the temperature dropped as we headed into the night hours. We stopped at the general store, grabbed some Pepsis, potato chips, and a few other snacks just in case we got hungry—which was a good probability since we planned to stay late into the morning hours.

Hammer drove close behind Gabe, and Gannon and I talked most of the journey. I knew the minute we arrived Hammer would beep the horn to alert Leela we were here. I hoped she would look out the window and see it was more than just me.

My heart thumped when we rounded the corner in Lamar and headed down the final stretch of road toward the apartments. Gabe slowed and pulled his car into the parking lot. Hammer followed and aligned us next to Gabe's station wagon. Gannon opened the door and stepped out, and I was right on his heels. When Hammer pressed the horn, a loud blaring sound rang out that startled everyone, including me.

Hammer stepped out to the crunch of gravel underfoot. "Sorry," he said sheepishly as the group looked in wonderment. We each carried a box of supplies to the front door, and once inside, we set up camp. I hoped Leela had heard the warning blast and took cover, remaining hidden until we left.

"I'd like to change things up tonight." Fang motioned with his head. "Gabe and Dee, first floor. Sam and Angel, second floor. Donnie and Gannon, the third floor."

"What?" I mumbled. I must have misunderstood.

"Sorry. You, me, and Hammer will start in the basement, and we'll rotate every hour. Sound fair?" Fang pointed to each group, and they all nodded their head in agreement.

"Wait, I thought I was the ghost magnet?" I pleaded to the group. "You said so yourself." I pointed to Fang.

"We're trying something different tonight. You okay with that?" Donnie sounded irritated.

I was only trying to protect my girl. I guess it was okay to call Leela my girl. *Well, maybe I was getting ahead of myself again.* I flashed back to Janice and Dee and smiled on the inside. I bobbed my head up and down. I felt defeated and sorry for Leela. Now she would have to hide for hours before I could see her—that's if she's even still here. I was hoping she was out tonight, but I was sure she was here with it being so cold.

The groups dispersed to their designated locations. Fang, Hammer, and I walked down the stairs. Hammer took his seat, and Fang played with the walkie-talkie, making sure everyone was in position. I paced about the basement, shining my light here and there until I noticed a concrete box in the corner. It was the size of a refrigerator, but broader. I looked closer. The top was made of wood, with hinges on each side. To my surprise, it was a door, so I lifted upward to reveal its contents. It was full of spring water. I dipped my hand in, the water cold on my fingers, and scooped a hand full to my mouth. It tasted delicious. I wasn't sure how the water tank stayed full, but it explained where Leela was getting her water.

I gently closed the lid and shined my light along the back wall. A clothesline cascaded through the rafters and a washboard sat in a small metal tub next to a faucet. For a building that was abandoned, this was amazing. I continued my search. There was a small pile of fresh-cut wood under an old gray tarp. I continued along the wall, my light stopping on a square-shaped frame a few feet from the floor. It was outlined like a picture frame, and after pushing and pulling, the door finally slid to the left. Bingo, this was what I was searching for—a dumb waiter.

I glanced at Fang and Hammer. They were busy; now was my chance. I turned and looked at the empty hole, and then I poked my head inside to look upward. My light stopped on the box some ten or fifteen above. I tugged on the rope, but it appeared jammed. I pulled harder to no avail. It was either stuck or secured in one location. I bet there was a station on every floor where you could access the box. If I had to guess, it was stuck between floors, which meant Leela must be hiding in the box. I was sure she was scared. I wanted to call out to her but couldn't. I closed the door as quietly as possible and moved a clothes rack in front to block the view, then looked over my shoulder. Hammer was writing something in the log, and Fang was playing with the cassette recorder. I quickly walked over to join them.

"Find anything interesting?" I detected something in Fang's voice. Had he seen me open the chamber?

"Nothing really," I whispered.

Hammer looked up. "What'd you find?"

I was never good at lying or keeping secrets. "It's a tank filled with spring water."

"They're pretty common around here," Fang added. He didn't move, nor did he appear shocked by my findings. I sighed with relief.

The first hour passed—no findings to report in the basement. We were now moving to the first floor. Donnie and Gannon said they recorded some weird sounds on the third floor, something we would have to listen to when we got back to Fang's. Sam and Angel were now on the third floor, alone again. I wasn't a hundred percent sure if they were in a relationship, but from how they looked together, I knew it was only a matter of time. I felt confident they wouldn't see anything strange. I felt like this was a complete waste of time, but I was trying to be patient and fair to the others. Hammer and I paced the corridor a few times, opening and closing all the doors. I sincerely looked for any signs of life, with nothing to report, I hate to say.

I hiked in the direction of the dumb waiter until I noticed the same framework on the wall. I rested my back against the wall. When the others were not looking, I pressed my ear firmly to the wall and lightly tapped on the wall. I didn't receive any response, so I banged a little stronger. A scratch, followed by another scratch, and then it went silent. My heart raced for a second. But it could have been a large insect or even a rat, and I wouldn't say I liked rats because they were filled with germs and diseases.

Another hour passed, and we made our way to the second floor. It was more of the same, nothing new. I grew hungry, so Hammer and I opened a bag of potato chips and split a bottle of Pepsi. I stared at my watch, only fifteen minutes to go, and we would be on the top floor. I could feel the electric current stirring inside of me.

Static, then a crackle from the radio. "Fang, Gerald?" Then there was silence. "Anyone there?"

"Copy." I noticed a level of excitement in Fang's voice. "Gabe, is everything alright?"

"Hurry."

Fang snatched his knapsack and darted for the stairs, Hammer grabbed the cassette recorder, and I followed with the camera dangling from my neck. We hurried up the final set of stairs. My nerves were a wreck. What if they found Leela? I couldn't imagine how she must feel, the fear of being hunted like an animal. I ran to her as fast as I could, skipping the last step and bouncing on the landing. Tripping over my own feet, I stumbled and landed on my hands and knees. I hopped to my feet, paying no attention to the searing pain in my left knee, and scrambled forward to join the others.

"I think I saw someone . . ." Gabe whispered.

"A guy or gal?" Fang asked, his voice riddled with excitement.

"A girl."

"A ghost?"

"No, well . . . maybe," Gabe stuttered. "I'm not sure."

"It was a girl," Dee added with certainty.

"Stay here." Fang stepped forward and slowly proceeded down the long hallway to where Dee was pointing. I mirrored each step Fang took.

"I got this," Fang whispered over his shoulder.

Desperation riddled my voice as I murmured, "Let me go first, please."

Fang hesitated but yielded, allowing me to take point. Fang followed close on my heels, with Hammer in tow and Gabe filming, and Dee behind him. I realized no one had followed his orders. That, I found amusing, then took a deep breath as I laid my hand on the last door on the left.

Adrenalin rushed through my veins. I worked up the nerve and slowly poked my head around the corner. I'd been in this room a few times. I had first spotted Leela here—this was her home and here we were, invading her space. I knew this was wrong. We were searching for ghosts, not a person. "Come on." Fang shoved me in the back, and I stumbled forward.

I stood in the doorway, and much to my surprise, the room was empty. I looked from side to side, nothing. I guess I expected Leela to be standing here. How silly was that? She must have ducked in the closet. "The room's empty," I announced.

Fang looked puzzled, then pushed me aside as he moved forward with Hammer close behind. They walked toward the closet. I could see his chest rising then falling. He was nervous; that was obvious. I'm sure Leela was too, as she was about to be discovered. Gabe and Dee pulled up alongside me. "Are you okay," Dee asked as she laid her hand on my arm. I twitched at first. I guess it was time to spill my guts.

"No, it's Leela," I sobbed. "She lives here." She had to be frightened. I wish I had told the group about Leela before today.

"Who's Leela?" Dee questioned, her voice soothing.

"I met her here some time ago. I think she's homeless. I've been helping her." The words flowed from my mouth. I felt a weight lift from my shoulders as I told my story to Dee. Then the panic stuck as Fang grabbed the closet handle and flung the door open with force. "Wait," I hollered. But it was too late, and the entrance lay open.

Fang threw his hands up in the air. "Another dead end." He paused, then turned to Gabe. "I thought you saw someone."

"I did, I mean we did!" He turned to Dee, his voice a bit uncertain as he added, "I thought we did?"

"Ah, yeah, she walked in here," Dee pointed.

"Well, there's no one here now," Fang exploded and threw his hands up. "I want so badly to prove to the world that ghosts exist."

"Calm down," Hammer cautioned, "we'll find her."

"Then she must be a ghost." I hoped this would draw their attention away from searching for Leela. Now I wondered if there was a false door, loose boards, or some escape hatch that Leela knew about.

"I saw a ghost." Gabe laughed. "I saw a real ghost!" He sounded so surprised with his accomplishment. "All by myself." Dee balled her hand and let it fly, striking Gabe in the arm. Shock and pain eased Gabe's smile. "That hurt."

"Excuse me. You mean *we* saw a ghost," she added.

"All right, guys, quiet down." Fang strutted back and forth, thinking about the situation. "It's time to rotate, so why don't you two stay at this end of the hallway, and the three of us will go to the other end and see if she returns." Fang pointed to Hammer and me.

Gabe blinked a few times as if he didn't hear Fang. "I found a ghost! I mean, we found her," Gabe corrected himself, and I noticed Dee smile.

"I'm happy for you," Fang conceded. "Spread out and search." Dee remained in the room, and Gabe ventured through the door across the hall. Fang beamed with confidence. I knew what he was thinking—today's the day. We were about to head to the other end of the hallway. "One more thing, let's get this on film." Fang pointed to Gabe and me. "Take as many pictures as you can."

We nodded in agreement, and I flicked the power button on.

"There!" My heart stopped at the sound of Fang's voice. I spun to catch a glimpse of Leela darting out of a room and down the corridor. "Wait!"

CHAPTER TWENTY-ONE

She dashed into one of the places on the right. I pivoted on my heels and gave chase. "Leela, wait. It's me, Gerald!" Leela was already at the other end of the hall. Man, she was fast! The excellent jump she had on me didn't help, either. Leela stopped, but only for a second to look over her shoulder, and then she turned, darting out of sight. I pursued her, my heart thumping so hard it hurt.

"Gerald!" I heard Fang cry as I gave chase.

"Stop!" Hammer screamed down the corridor, but I continued.

I had only found her a month ago and wasn't about to lose her now. I needed to explain why I brought this group of people to her home. I couldn't even imagine how she must feel about me at the moment, but I knew betrayed would be a good start.

I wished I'd told Fang and the rest of the gang about Leela before we arrived. Maybe I could have prevented this. How could I have been so stupid? Now it was too late. So why second guess myself? I plowed forward and grabbed the door frame, rounding the corner. I could hear everyone screaming for me to stop, but I had to explain to Leela that we mean her no harm. Shock riddled my face as I continued my chase, and the next thing I knew . . . I was flying!

No.

I was falling.

I was hurtling down the long, empty elevator shaft; my arms flailing at my sides. I had been in such a hurry to catch up with Leela that I'd forgotten there were no doors and no elevator car to stop me. Now it was too late as I plummeted four floors to the basement.

They say everything slows down when you're about to have a car accident. The thing is, I guess that applies to all accidents.

I thought about my childhood, missing my father, always wondering what it would have been like to come home from school to see him waiting for me as my mother would, to read together, play catch, or take long walks and talk about this and that. The sad truth was, I didn't remember my father.

My mind raced to my mother. She worked so hard to give me all the things I had, and how she sacrificed so much to have the tools I needed to succeed. All the Christmases we spent together, the birthdays, and the day I won the local spelling bee contest—she was always by my side. I felt horrible for not staying longer this past Christmas. What I'd give to spend another day with her smiling and being strong for me like she always was.

Then there's Hammer, who protected me from the bullies, who I tutored through high school and helped with his homework. What started as a business relationship turned into friendship. He truly was my best friend. I thought about Gannon and how we shared so many things in common and how I couldn't imagine life without him.

A vision of Dee and Angel floated before me—two incomparable beauties who were always nice and understanding. Who could ask for better friends, even when I was a brat and being obnoxious? And of course, Fang and the rest of the ghost hunters. They have all given me so much joy. I am truly blessed.

I guess this is what it would be like if I were in outer space and about to be sucked into a black hole. How could I be so smart yet so foolish to forget about the empty elevator shaft? I've been in this building numerous times, night and day. However, here I was, falling and about to feel the crunch of the concrete floor below.

I don't remember making any sound when I collided with the floor. I only felt the wind escape my lungs, and I noticed stars and butterflies floating above my vision. It reminded me of the first time I got punched in the gut.

I felt twisted like a Bavarian pretzel. I couldn't feel my arms or legs. I thought one might be pinned underneath me, and the other was next to me. The room began to spin. I felt nauseous. And then the pain seared, taking over my body.

I was losing feeling everywhere and my mind began to fade. Another memory surfaced. I was not too fond of carnival rides since they made me sick, but I rode one when I was young. Mom had put me on the merry-go-round where the horses were painted in elegant colors. But once we started to move, my lunch spilled all over the horse. At this moment, I felt the same way. I wanted to barf. Only this time, I didn't have the strength to do so.

I woke to the sound of voices. I heard someone call my name. I managed to open my eyes. Hammer stood over me, and tears traced his cheeks. "I'm so sorry," he mouthed to me. I'd never seen him cry. I watched Angel's lips move, but she didn't say anything. *She does look like an angel from this view*. I closed my eyes, hoping this was all a bad dream, but the pain intensified. Time was marching along at a snail's pace. I wasn't sure how long I laid at the bottom of the elevator shaft . . . *Why hasn't Leela showed up, or maybe she had, but I didn't notice? I was sure she'd introduced herself by now. How long have I been lying here?*

Fang tried to comfort me. I felt something soft under my head when Fang placed a blanket under me. I cracked a wry smile. Strange voices echoed, and someone approached—a voice I didn't recognize. "Give us room please." I tried to lean forward but couldn't. "Step aside. Move out of the way."

A blurry vision of a man appeared before me. "Gerald, can you hear me?" He waved something in front of me.

"Get the damn light out of my eyes," I yelled, but no words escaped. I wasn't sure I even said anything. *I'm . . . confused.* I tilted my head slightly to one side. I blinked a few times to let him know I understood. I spotted red flashing lights dance on the walls. I saw Hammer, Fang, and Gannon huddled in the corner. They look scared. *Did they know something I didn't?*

Had it been minutes or hours? I couldn't tell anymore. Did someone call for help? Who were they talking to? Was that a cop? It looked like that from here. I noticed his shiny badge. My eyes darted about, and I saw Gabe comforting Dee, who appeared to be crying. I spotted Sam, Donnie, and Angel, who looked like they've been crying, too. I think I'm the only one who's not crying. Maybe because I was in so much pain. Was I going to be alright? Did I look worse than I felt? What's going to happen to me? I'm sure I'll be fine . . . at least, I hoped so, for my mother's sake.

I couldn't feel anything as the paramedics turned me on my side. Something hard slid under me, and I thought it was a large board. I was glad I could feel that on my back. Now they were doing something to my legs, my head, and my waist. *Oh*, I believe they were straps. I lay on my back, looking at the darkness above. A man's face appeared once again, and another guy stood at my feet. "We're going to lift you now, one, two, and three." I jolted upward, and we bounced up the stairs. Finally, I didn't feel any pain. Maybe it was the needle they shoved in my arm.

We arrived on the main floor and I watched the ceiling roll past. I never noticed before the large wooden beams that crisscrossed, making a pattern on the ceiling. It was kind of nice. And was that hand-carved wood? I don't see Leela. I'm sure she feels horrible, maybe even a bit guilty for letting this happen to me. I'd done so much to help her, and if she were standing there, I'd have let her know this wasn't her fault. She must have hidden in the room before the empty shaft. After all, it was dark, and my light had been bouncing on the walls as I ran.

The mistake would have been easy for anyone to make, especially me. I'd always been kind of clumsy. We stopped moving. The man laid something over me; why did he cover my eyes? The blanket moved and I could see again. *Oh*, they scared me for a second. I noticed the stars above in the night sky and the clouds rolled past at a quick pace. I felt a tinge of coldness in my feet, something I thought was a good sign.

Hammer ran toward me. "You're going to be just fine, you hear me, Gerald Dupickle?" Two cops held him back as the paramedics rushed me forward. He's crying, kicking, and screaming. Gannon and Fang look away like they can't bear to watch.

I faded out, only to wake and see the plush white covering of the ambulance walls. A doctor and nurse hovered over me. I could tell the vehicle was moving. I was thrilled my senses were still working. I need to hang on until I got to the hospital. I blinked in and out a few times during our journey. The ambulance came to a halt, the door opened wide, and they slid the gurney out and placed me on another table. An older gentleman hovered over me. He had bags under his droopy eyes. His hair was sparkling white and his chin long. Had he had any sleep? I felt bad for waking him in the middle of the night, to have pulled him away from his family at such a late hour. He whispered something in my ear that I didn't hear or understand. "Are you God?" I squeezed out. *Are you here to take me to Heaven?* I thought my lips moved, but I couldn't be sure. Maybe this was all happening inside my head. Fatigue set in, and I closed my eyes. I flashed back to me sitting on the front porch. Now I understood how the worm felt before being devoured.

CHAPTER TWENTY-TWO

My memory faded in and out as I struggled to remember the past few months. I opened my eyes; I must have dozed off again. I heard the sound of birds chirping in the distance. The sunshine beaming through the window warmed my cheek. It's springtime or early summer, one of my favorite times of the year—the flowers were in full bloom while the birds and animals hustled around. I gazed out the window to my west to watch the sun set. Another beautiful day had come to a close.

I looked across the vacant room. Leela smiled and stared back at me. Her eyes glistening as the sun reflected off her skin. Her blonde hair toppled over her shoulders to the midway point of her back. Her hand rested on her cheek, then moved upward, and I watched her fingers intertwine as she twirled the strands of her hair. I knew she was someone special because she's never left my side since that day. I was impressed with her dedication to me, and I hoped she knew how much that meant to me.

She waltzed over to me and snuggled close. A small smile escaped as I unwrapped our sandwiches, our eyes locking. I loved the peaceful moments we shared. She divided a bottle of Pepsi into two Styrofoam cups. That was one more thing we had in common—our love for Pepsi. I couldn't think of another soda pop I enjoyed as much. The sandwich melted in my mouth, and we grinned with our mouths full and shared a laugh. I didn't have a care in the world when I was next to Leela.

I caught the last glimpse of the sun setting behind the mountain. The light faded, leaving only the moonlight cascading through the window. We sat in silence. I moved my hand to hers and she embraced it, dipping the side of her face to rest on my shoulder. My heart warmed.

I still struggled with moments like these, but I was confident this was the right time. I knew I was young, but I could provide for us with my book sales and a college degree. I wanted to spend my life with her. I know I've thought this way about other girls in the past, but this was different. Leela was different. We shared this special connection that no words could describe. We were meant to be together. I felt ready to move forward in our relationship. So today was the day I would ask. No, I didn't have a ring, but did that really matter when two people shared something as unique as we did?

I knew my mother would disapprove, and possibly Hammer too, but it didn't matter. I'd made up my mind, and no one was going to change it.

"Leela."

"Yes." Her brown eyes met mine, and she smiled.

I was nervous, and I didn't know how to ask this question. I opened my mouth, but no words escaped. "Ah, why are we sitting in the dark?"

"Where else would we be?" The clouds outside moved and the moonlight beamed to illuminate the room.

"I was thinking . . ." I couldn't believe how scared I was. It was a straightforward question. The butterflies had returned to my stomach, and I thought I was going to throw up. But I needed to ask her. I was sure she would say yes.

Okay, I was *hoping* she would say yes.

Suddenly her gaze moved to the door. The creak of the floorboard caught our attention. I rotated my head and noticed a small beam of light in the corridor. For a second, I thought I imagined it, but the light continued to move. We had company. I shuffled to my feet to shield Leela, who stood peering over my shoulder.

The light grew brighter. I thought I knew who it might be. Fang and the group must have followed me. If that was true, I was going to have to give them a piece of my mind. They had no right spying on me. What I did with my life was up to me. I didn't feel sorry for leaving the group, but I thought they had understood. After the accident, I couldn't go back to ghost hunting. I needed to do something meaningful and spend precious time with those who meant the most to me. I wasn't trying to ditch my friends for good; I only wanted to balance my time between them and Leela.

Shuffling footsteps grew closer and my mind raced. What if it wasn't Fang and the gang? Then what would I do? After all, we were trespassing. I knew we were trapped with no place to hide, but I was done hiding. And so, I decided to stand my ground, even as the light cascaded through the doorway. We braced ourselves. I stood ready to confront whoever was about to invade our space. Leela stood at my side, and she placed a hand on my shoulder. My confidence soared.

The beam of light entered the room. I couldn't make out the faces from the glare shining directly at me, but the voices I heard had a familiar ring to them.

"Do you mind shining the light in the other direction?" The words came out harsher than I expected.

No one responded as a second light entered the room, the beams crisscrossing as if searching for something. My anger boiled as I recognized Donnie and Fang. A third person appeared . . . Hammer.

"What the hell, guys?" I threw my arms in the air with disgust.

"Did you feel that?" Fang whispered to Donnie.

"I did."

"Get out," I screamed again, growing frustrated. I knelt forward, grabbed my cup, and launched it toward the guys. I watched as the cup hurtled in the air.

The boys ducked and pushed themselves against the wall. A bright flash of light followed. "I think I got it," Hammer murmured, staring at the picture in his hands.

I stepped forward with Leela sticking to my side like glue. "Run through them," she whispered in my ear.

"What?" I turned to Leela, confused. She nudged me forward.

I shook my head, and instead, I tried a different approach. "Guys . . . guys?" I threw my hands in the air and watched as they stepped back.

“Did you feel that?” Hammer asked.

“I sure did.” Fang stepped back as a gust of wind rushed over him.

Leela whispered something in my ear again. I was confused. “What do you mean run through them? You mean, push them out of the way? Right . . .” I chuckled. “If you haven’t noticed, they’re bigger than me.”

“No, silly.” She giggled. “Like this.” She pushed between them and out into the hallway. She spun on her heels and motioned me to follow. I was baffled. I couldn’t wrap my mind around what Leela was asking me to do. Panic set in and I felt like I was going to hyperventilate. I sank to the floor. Leela was back at my side before I could blink. She wrapped her arm around my head and instructed me to relax.

“Take a deep breath, my love.” She stroked the back of my neck.

“What?” The air rushed out of my lungs, not because of the events unfolding around me, but all because of one word. Love. “Did . . . did you just . . . say . . . love?” I smiled, and my heart exploded with joy. I was rendered speechless. We felt the same about each other. I found my courage and bounced to my feet, tossing my arms out, and yelled to the guys, “Back off!”

Their eyes widened as they flew backward and into the wall. The three of them slowly drifted to the floor. “That was groovy.” Fang smiled as he, Hammer, and Donnie got back to their feet. “Show yourself,” Fang demanded.

My eyes darted to each of them. "What are you talking about?" Leela laid a soft hand on my shoulder and pressed her face to my back; her warmth was running through me. I began to feel funny. *Was this what being in love felt like?*

"It . . . it's . . . you," Fang stuttered, and I noticed a tear run down the side of his cheek. "I'm so sorry, man." He trembled. "I didn't do enough to protect you. Can you ever forgive me?" He cupped his hands over his eyes and began to sob as he lowered himself to his knees.

"No way," Donnie choked out as his eyes bulged.

"It can't be." Hammer's jaw dropped open. "Gerald?" Several tears traced down his cheek. "Is that you?" He sank to the floor and stared at me like he'd seen a ghost.

"Of course, it's me. Who do you think it is?"

"They couldn't see you before, Gerald." Leela squeezed my shoulder. "I'm using my strength to make you visible." Leela's voice was calm in my ear.

"I'm confused, I-I . . . don't understand." *What does she mean they can't see me?* My knees gave out, and I puddled to the floor. Leela was rubbing my head and holding me tight. Hammer knelt next to me with Fang and Donnie looking on.

For a smart guy, I could be slow at times. I flashed back to that cold winter night in January. I chased Leela down the hallway, fell in the empty elevator shaft, and was rushed to the hospital. It seemed like a lifetime ago.

"How could you let this happen?" I pushed away from Leela.

"I didn't realize until it was too late. I never meant for anyone to get hurt, especially you, Gerald. You were the only one who was kind and cared for me," Leela pleaded.

"How could you not tell me?"

"I thought you knew."

"What about the food I left for you?"

"Kids play in this building in the daytime, haven't you noticed?" Her eyes grew wide, and her face was riddled with fear. I swallowed bitterly but softened and extended my arms toward her.

She embraced me and whispered, "I'm sorry. I never meant to deceive you."

"I just feel lost. It's too much to take in."

"I'm here for you." She snuggled into me, and I was glad to have her by my side.

We sat in silence before Hammer cut in, "Hey, buddy," he wiped a tear from his cheek, "I'm sorry I wasn't able to stop this from happening. It's all my fault. I miss you so much."

"It can't be . . ." I looked at Hammer, Fang, and Donnie before I finally began to cry. Everything was starting to make sense, but I didn't want to accept the truth. "How's my mom?" I blubbered out.

I'd never seen the big guy cry so hard. He opened his mouth several times but only cried more. He finally coughed out the word, "Better."

"Tell her I love her and miss her." The words tumbled out of my mouth.

Hammer bobbed his head and wiped a few more tears from his cheek.

"I should have stopped." My words were hard to understand. "But I kept running and look at me now."

The hours passed, and we sat and stared at each other, exchanging a few words here and there. Just when we thought we were done crying, we cried some more.

"I know how you feel. I felt the same way when this happened to me," Leela whispered. I cupped her hand in mine.

"How did you know?" I gazed at Hammer, Donnie, then Fang.

"Donnie and I did some digging at the library. We even drove to the big library at the state college and spent the entire day until we found an article about a seventeen-year-old girl who lived here and went missing in the woods. They never found her. Her name was Leela Partridge."

"I miss my parents," she wept. I draped my arm around Leela.

"We realized the Leela you spoke of that night was not a living girl. She had to be a ghost, and we thought if she lived here, then maybe you would, too." Fang frowned and mouthed the word sorry to me again.

"Where's Gannon?"

"He couldn't . . . He gave up ghost hunting after that night, and so did the others." Hammer paused to take a deep breath. "Matter of fact, so had I, until Fang called. His theory ate at me until I couldn't take it anymore, and I just had to know the truth. Were you still here? Could I see you again? Could you forgive me? I just had to know, and I wondered, what if they were right?" Hammer cracked a little smile.

"I'm glad you came." I wiped away a tear. I reached out to hug him, and my body passed through him. I watched and smiled as he shivered on the floor.

I guess in the end, I got exactly what I was looking for—love and great friends. It's not how I envisioned it, but I know Leela and I will be happy, and the guys can come visit whenever they like.

Acknowledgments

I'm a writer, so I mostly work alone. I greatly appreciate my wife Toni for putting up with my weird ways and allowing me the time I needed to complete this story.

Thank you to my daughter Jessica for working with me on this project. I valued all your suggestions, ideas and criticism throughout the writing process.

Special thanks to my Editor Silvia Curry for your sharp eye and helpful hints. I couldn't have done this without you. You took my manuscript and added your magical touch to make this story what it is today.

Silvia Curry at Silvia's Reading Corner
www.silviasreading.webs.com

Thank you, PhoenixWhirl, Melissa Derr, and Scott Hall for finding those elusive mistakes that drive readers nuts. Along with all your thoughts and suggestions during the proofreading process.

Thank you to all the Alpha readers. Linda Spann, Carolyn Hornick, Teresa Thompson, and Alexis Stencil. For taking time out of your day to read my story and tell me what worked and what didn't.

Thank you to Cheryl Haller at B&N for taking a chance on me and allowing my books in the Tampa area stores.

Steve Altier is an award-winning young adult mystery and suspense author. He was born in a small town in central Pennsylvania. Aka “Lizardville.”

He now resides in Tampa with his wife Toni. Steve has four loving daughters and a house full of cats.

He enjoys writing, reading, bowling, and spending time at amusement parks. He loves to travel, take trips to the beach, or laying around the pool with family and friends.

Learn more about Steve and his stories by following him on social media or visit his website. www.stevealtier.com

Steve would love to hear from you. You can drop him a line at **stevealtierbooks@outlook.com**

CPSIA information can be obtained
at www.ICGtesting.com
Printed in the USA
BVHW031457310821
615696BV00007B/178